ALMOND

ALMOND

A NOVEL

WON-PYUNG SOHN

TRANSLATED FROM THE KOREAN BY SANDY JOOSUN LEE

HARPERVIA

An Imprint of HarperCollins*Publishers*

HarperCollins books may be purchased for educational, business, or sales promotional use. For information, please email the Special Markets Department at SPsales@ harpercollins.com.

Originally published as 아몬드 in South Korea in 2017 by Changbi Publishers.

FIRST EDITION

Designed by SBI Book Arts, LLC

Library of Congress Cataloging-in-Publication Data

Names: Son, Wŏn-p'yŏng, 1979- author. I Lee, Joosun, translator.
Title: Almond : a novel / Won-Pyung Sohn, Joosun Lee.

Other titles: Amondŭ. English
Description: First edition. I New York : HarperCollins, 2020. I
Identifiers: LCCN 2019044008 (print) I LCCN 2019044009 (ebook) I ISBN 9780062961372 (hardcover) I ISBN 9780062961402 (ebook)
Classification: LCC PL994.77.W66 A87 2020 (print) I LCC PL994.77.W66 (ebook) I DDC 895.73/5—dc23
LC record available at https://lccn.loc.gov/2019044008
LC ebook record available at https://lccn.loc.gov/2019044009

ISBN 978-0-06-296137-2
ISBN 978-0-06-304146-2 (ANZ)

20 21 22 23 24 LSC 10 9 8 7 6 5 4 3 2 1

Notes

- Alexithymia, or the inability to identify and express one's feelings, is a mental disorder first described in medical journals in the 1970s. Its known causes are lack of emotional development during a person's early childhood, post-traumatic stress disorder, and the smaller inborn amygdalae, in which case, fear is the emotion these parts of the brain are least able to identify and express. Recently, however, new studies have suggested that the ability of the amygdalae to process fear and anxiety can be increased through training. This novel describes alexithymia based on these studies, and with the author's imagination.
- P. J. Nolan is a fictional character.
- The dinosaurs' sizes mentioned in this novel are based on Bernard Most's *The Littlest Dinosaurs*. Their actual sizes may differ based on various studies.

TO DAN

PROLOGUE

I have almonds inside me.
So do you.
So do those you love and those you hate.
No one can feel them.
You just know they are there.
This story is, in short, about a monster meeting another
monster. One of the monsters is me.

I won't tell you whether it has a happy ending or a tragic ending.

Because, first of all, every story becomes boring once the ending is spoiled.

Second of all, not telling you will make you more engaged in this one.

Lastly, and I know it sounds like an excuse, but neither you nor I nor anyone can ever really know whether a story is happy or tragic.

PART ONE

1

Six were dead, and one was wounded that day. First were Mom and Granny. Then a college student who had rushed in to stop the man. Then two men in their fifties who had stood in the front rank of the Salvation Army parade, followed by a policeman. Finally, the man himself. He had chosen to be the last victim of his manic bloodshed. He stabbed himself in the chest hard and, like most of the other victims, died before the ambulance came. I simply watched the whole thing unfold before me.

Just standing there with blank eyes, as always.

2

The first incident happened when I was six. The symptoms had been there way earlier, but it was then that they had finally risen to the surface. That day, Mom must've forgotten to come get me from kindergarten. She told me later that she had gone to see Dad after all these years, to tell him that she would finally let him go, not that she would meet someone new or anything, but that she would move on anyway. Apparently, she had said all that to him as she wiped the faded walls of his mausoleum. Meanwhile, as her love came to an end once and for all, I, the uninvited guest of their young love, was being completely forgotten.

After all the kids were gone, I wandered out of the kindergarten on my own. All that six-year-old me could remember about his house was that it was somewhere over a bridge. I went up and stood on the overpass with my head hanging over the railing. I saw cars gliding by beneath me. It reminded me of something I had seen somewhere, so I gathered as much saliva as possible in my mouth. I took aim at a car and spat. My spit evaporated long before it hit the car, but I kept my eyes on the road and kept spitting until I felt dizzy.

"What are you doing! That's disgusting!"

I looked up to see a middle-aged woman passing by, glaring

at me, then she just continued on her way, gliding past me like the cars below, and I was left alone again. The stairways from the overpass fanned out in every direction. I lost my bearings. The world I saw underneath the stairs was all the same icy gray, left and right. A couple of pigeons flapped away above my head. I decided to follow them.

By the time I realized I was going the wrong way, I'd already gone too far. At kindergarten, I'd been learning a song called "Go Marching." *Earth is round, go go march ahead*, and just like the lyrics, I thought that, somehow, I would eventually get to my house if I'd just *go go march ahead*. I stubbornly continued my small steps forward.

The main road led to a narrow alley lined by old houses, those crumbling walls all marked with crimson, random numbers and the word "vacant." There was no one in sight. Suddenly, I heard someone cry out, *Ah*, in a low voice. Not sure if it was *Ah* or *Uh*. Maybe it was *Argh*. It was a low, short cry. I walked toward the sound, and it grew as I approached closer and closer, then it changed to *Urgh* and *Eeeh*. It was coming from around the corner. I turned the corner without hesitation.

A boy was lying on the ground. A small boy whose age I couldn't tell, but then black shadows were being cast on and off him again and again. He was being beaten. The short cries weren't coming from him but from the shadows surrounding him, more like shouts of exertion. They kicked and spat at him. I later learned that they were only middle school students, but back then, those shadows seemed tall and huge like grown-ups.

The boy didn't resist or even make a sound, as if he'd grown used to the beating. He was getting tossed back and forth like a rag doll. One of the shadows kicked the boy in the side as a final blow. Then they left. The boy was covered in blood, like a coat of red paint. I approached him. He looked older than me, maybe eleven or twelve years old, around twice my age. But I still felt like he was younger than me. His chest was heaving quickly, his breath short and shallow like a newborn puppy's. It was obvious he was in danger.

I went back to the alley. It was still empty—only the red letters on the gray walls disturbed my eyes. After wandering for quite some time, I finally saw a small corner store. I slid open the door and stepped inside.

"Excuse me."

Family Game was on television. The shopkeeper was snickering so hard watching the show that he must not have heard me. The guests in the show were playing a game where one person wearing earplugs had to guess words by watching others mouth them. The word was "trepidation." I have no idea why I still remember the word. I didn't even know what it meant then. One lady kept making wrong guesses and drew laughs from the audience and the shopkeeper. Eventually, time ran out, and her team lost. The shopkeeper smacked his lips, maybe because he felt bad for her.

"Sir," I called to him again.

"Yes?" He finally turned.

"There's someone lying in the alley."

"Really?" he said indifferently and sat up.

On television, both teams were about to play another round of a high-points game that could turn the tide.

"He could die," I said, fiddling with one of the chewy caramel packs neatly lined up on the display stand.

"Is that so?"

"Yes, I'm sure." That was when he finally looked me in the eye.

"Where'd you learn to say such creepy things? Lying is bad, son."

I fell silent for a while, trying to find the words to convince him. But I was too young to have much vocabulary, and I couldn't think of anything else truer than what I had already said.

"He could die soon."

All I could do was repeat myself.

$$3$$

I waited for the show to finish while the shopkeeper called the police. When he saw me fiddling with the caramel again, he snapped at me to leave if I wasn't going to buy anything. The police took their time coming to the scene—but all I could think of was the boy lying on the cold ground. He was already dead.

The thing is, he was the shopkeeper's son.

———

I sat on a bench at the police station, swinging my legs hovering in the air. They went back and forth, working up a cool breeze. It was already dark, and I felt sleepy. Just as I was about to doze off, the police station door swung open to reveal Mom. She let out a cry when she saw me and stroked my head so hard it hurt. Before she could fully enjoy the moment of our reunion, the door swung wide open again and in came the shopkeeper, his body held up by policemen. He was wailing, his face covered in tears. His expression was quite different from when he had watched TV earlier. He slumped down on his knees, trembling, and punched the ground. Suddenly he got to his feet and yelled, pointing his finger at me. I couldn't exactly understand his rambling, but what I got was something like this:

"You should've said it seriously, now it's too late for my son!"

The policeman next to me shrugged. "What would a kinder-gartener know," he said, and managed to stop the shopkeeper from sinking to the floor. I couldn't agree with the shopkeeper though. I'd been perfectly serious all along. Never once did I smile or over-react. I couldn't understand why he was scolding me for that, but six-year-old me didn't know the words needed to form this question into a full sentence, so I just stayed silent. Instead, Mom raised her voice for me, turning the police station into a mad-house, with the clamoring of a parent who'd lost his child and a parent who'd found hers.

That night, I played with toy blocks as I always did. They were in the shape of a giraffe and could be changed into an elephant if I twisted down its long neck. I felt Mom staring at me, her eyes scanning every part of my body.

"Weren't you scared?" she asked.

"No," I said.

Rumors about that incident—specifically, how I didn't even blink at the sight of someone being beaten to death—spread quickly. From then on, Mom's fears became a reality one after another.

Things got worse after I entered elementary school. One day, on the way home from school, a girl walking in front of me tripped over a rock. She was blocking my way, so I examined the Mickey Mouse hairband she was wearing while I waited for her to get back up. But she just sat there and cried. Finally, her mom came and helped her stand. She glanced at me, clucking her tongue.

"You see your friend fall and don't even ask if she's okay? So the rumors are true, something *is* weird about you."

I couldn't think of anything to say, so I said nothing. The other kids sensed that something was happening and gathered around me, their whispers prickling my ears. For all I knew, they were probably echoing what the girl's mom had said. That was when Granny came in to save me, appearing out of nowhere like Wonder Woman, sweeping me up into her arms.

"Watch your mouth!" she snapped in her husky voice. "She was just unlucky to trip. Who do you think you are to blame my boy?"

Granny didn't forget to say a word to the kids, either.

"What are you staring at, you little brats?"

When we walked farther away, I looked up to see Granny with her lips pressed tight.

"Granny, why do people call me weird?"

Her lips loosened.

"Maybe it's because you're special. People just can't stand it when something is different, *eigoo*, my adorable little monster."

Granny hugged me so tight my ribs hurt. She always called me a monster. To her, that wasn't a bad thing.

4

To be honest, it took me a while to understand the nickname Granny had so affectionately given me. Monsters in books weren't adorable. In fact, monsters were completely opposite to everything adorable. I wondered why she'd call me that. Even after I learned the word "paradox"—which meant putting contradictory ideas together—I was confused. Did the stress fall on "adorable" or "monster?" Anyway, she said she called me that out of love, so I decided to trust her.

Tears welled up in Mom's eyes as Granny told her about the Mickey Mouse girl.

"I knew this day would come . . . I just didn't expect it to be this soon . . ."

"Oh, stop that nonsense! If you want to whine, go whine in your room and keep the door shut!"

That stopped Mom's crying for a moment. She glanced at Granny, a bit startled by the sudden outburst. Then she began to cry even harder. Granny clucked her tongue and shook her head, her eyes resting on a corner of the ceiling, heaving a deep sigh. This seemed to be their typical routine.

It was true, Mom had been worried about me for a long time.

That was because I was always different from other kids—
different from birth even, because:

I never smiled.

At first, Mom had thought I was just slow to develop. But
parenting books told her that a baby starts smiling three days
after being born. She counted the days—it had been nearly a
hundred.

Like a fairy-tale princess cursed to never smile, I didn't bat
an eye. And like a prince from a faraway land trying to win over
his beloved's heart, Mom tried everything. She tried clapping,
bought different colored rattles, and even did silly dances to
children's songs. When she wore herself out, she went out to the
veranda and smoked, a habit she'd barely managed to quit after
finding out she was pregnant with me. I once saw a video filmed
around that time, where Mom was trying so hard, and I was just
staring at her. My eyes were too deep and calm to be those of a
child's. Whatever she did, Mom couldn't make me smile.

The doctor said I had no particular issues. Except for the lack
of smiles, the test results showed that my height, weight, and
behavioral development were all normal for my age. The pediatri-
cian in our neighborhood dismissed Mom's concerns, telling her
not to worry, because her baby was growing just fine. For a while
after that, Mom tried to comfort herself by saying that I was just
a little quieter than other kids.

Then something happened around my first birthday, which
proved that she'd been right to worry.

That day, Mom had put a red kettle filled with hot water on the
table. She turned her back to mix the powdered milk. I reached

for the kettle and it fell from the table, tumbling down to the floor, splashing hot water everywhere. I still have a faint burn mark like a medal from that day. I screamed and cried. Mom thought I'd be scared of water or red kettles from that point on, like a normal kid would be. But I wasn't. I was afraid of neither water nor kettles. I kept reaching for the red kettle whenever I saw it, whether it had cold or hot water inside.

The evidence kept adding up. There was a one-eyed old man who lived downstairs with a big black dog he always kept tied to the post in the yard. I stared straight into the old man's milky-white pupils without fear, and when Mom lost track of me for a moment, I reached out to touch his dog, who bared his teeth and growled. Even after seeing the kid next door, bitten and bleeding from doing the very same thing, I did it again. Mom had to con-stantly intervene.

After several incidents like this, Mom started worrying that I might have a low IQ, but there was no other proof of that. So, like any mother, she tried to find a way to cast her doubts about her child in a positive light.

He's just more fearless than other kids.

That was how she described me in her diary.

———

Even so, any mother's anxiety would peak if their child hadn't smiled by their fourth birthday. Mom held my hand and took me to a bigger hospital. That day is the first memory carved into my brain. It's blurry, as if I were watching from underwater, but comes into sharp focus every once in a while, like this:

A man in a white lab coat sits in front of me. Beaming, he starts showing me different toys one by one. Some of them he shakes. Then he taps my knee with a small hammer. My leg swings up higher than I thought possible. He then puts his fingers under my armpits. It tickles, and I giggle a little. Then he takes out photographs and asks me some questions. One of the pictures I still remember vividly.

"The kid in this photo is crying because his mommy is gone. How would he feel?"

Not knowing the answer, I look up to Mom sitting next to me. She smiles at me and strokes my hair, then subtly bites her lower lip.

———

A few days later, Mom takes me somewhere else, saying I will get to ride a spaceship, but we end up at another hospital. I ask her why she brings me here when I'm not even sick, but she doesn't answer.

Inside, I'm told to lie down on something cold. I'm sucked into a white tank. *Beep beep beep.* I hear strange sounds. My boring space trip ends there.

Then the scene changes. I suddenly see many more men in white lab coats. The oldest among them hands me a blurry black-and-white photograph, saying that it's the inside of my head. What a liar. That's clearly not my head. But Mom keeps nodding as if she believes such an obvious lie. Whenever the old guy opens his mouth, the younger guys around him take notes. Eventually, I start to get a little bored and fidget with my feet, kicking at the old man's desk. When Mom puts her hand on my shoulder to stop me, I look up and see that she's crying.

All I can remember about the rest of that day is Mom's crying. She cries and cries and cries. She's still crying when we head back to the waiting room. There is a cartoon playing on TV, but I can't focus because of her. The defender of the universe is fighting off the bad guy, but all she does is cry. Finally, an old man dozing off next to me wakes up and barks at her, "Stop acting miserable, you noisy woman, I've had enough!" It works. Mom purses her lips tight like a scolded teenager, silently trembling.

5

Mom fed me a lot of almonds. I've tried almonds from America, Australia, China, and Russia. All the countries that export them to Korea. The Chinese ones had a bitter, awful taste, and the Australian ones tasted kind of sour and earthy. There are the Korean ones too, but my favorite are the American ones, especially the ones from California. They have a soft brown hue from absorbing the blazing sunlight there.

Now I will tell you my secret how to eat them.

First, you hold the package and feel the shape of the almonds from the outside. You need to feel the hard, stubborn kernels with your fingers. Next, you slowly tear the top part of the package and open the double zipper. Then, you poke your nose inside the package and slowly breathe in. You have to close your eyes for this part. You take it lightly, occasionally holding your breath, to allow as much time as possible for the scent to reach the body. Finally, when the scent fills you up from deep inside, you pop half a handful of them into your mouth. Roll them around in there for a while and feel their texture. Poke the pointy parts with your tongue. Feel the grooves on their surface. You have to make sure not to take too long. If they get bloated from your saliva, they will taste bad. These steps are all just a lead-up to the finale. If too short, it will be dull. Too long and the impact will be gone. You have to find the right timing for yourself. You have to imagine the almonds getting bigger—from the size of a fingernail to the size of a grape, a kiwi, an orange, then a watermelon. Finally the size of a rugby ball. That's the moment. *Crunch*, you crush them. You will taste the sunshine all the way from California, flooding right into your mouth.

The reason I bother going through this ritual is not because I like almonds. At every meal of the day, there were almonds on the table. There was no way of getting around them. So I just made up a way to eat them. Mom thought that if I ate a lot of almonds, the almonds inside my head would get bigger. It was one of the very few hopes she clung to.

Everybody has two almonds inside their head, stuck firmly on somewhere between the back of your ears and the back of your skull. In fact, they're called "amygdalae," derived from the Latin word for almond because their size and shape are exactly like one.

When you get stimulated by something outside your body, these almonds send signals into your brain. Depending on the type of stimulation, you'll feel fear or anger, joy or sorrow.

But for some reason, my almonds don't seem to work well. They don't really light up when they are stimulated. So I don't know why people laugh or cry. Joy, sorrow, love, fear—all these things are vague ideas to me. The words "emotion" and "empathy" are just meaningless letters in print.

6

The doctors diagnosed me with alexithymia, or the inability to express your feelings. They figured that I was too young, my symptoms different from Asperger's syndrome, and my other developments didn't show signs of autism. It's not necessarily that I was unable to express feelings, but more that I was unable to identify them in the first place. I didn't have a problem with making sentences or understanding them like people who'd damaged the Broca or Wernicke areas in the brain, which dealt with primary speech functions. But I couldn't feel emotions, couldn't identify other people's feelings, and got confused over the names of emotions. The doctors all said it was because the almonds inside my head, the amygdalae, were unusually small and the contact between the limbic system and the frontal lobe didn't function as smoothly as it should.

One of the symptoms of having small amygdalae is that you don't know how it feels to be afraid. People sometimes say how cool it'd be to be fearless, but they don't know what they're talking about. Fear is an instinctive defense mechanism necessary for survival. Not knowing fear doesn't mean that you're brave; it means you're stupid enough to stay standing on the road when a car is charging toward you. I was even more unlucky. On top of my lack of fear, I was limited in all my emotional functions. The only silver lining, the doctors said, was that my intelligence wasn't affected despite having such small amygdalae.

They advised that, since everyone has different brains, we should see how things go. Some of them made rather tempting offers, saying that I could play a big role in uncovering the mysteries of the brain. Researchers at university hospitals proposed long-term research projects on my growth, to be reported in medical journals. There would be generous compensation for taking part, and depending on the research results, an area of the brain might even be named after me, like the Broca area or Wernicke area. The Seon Yunjae area. But the doctors were met with a flat refusal from Mom, who was already sick of them.

For one thing, Mom knew Broca and Wernicke were scientists, not patients. She had read all kinds of books about the brain from her regular visits to the local library. She also didn't like that the doctors saw me as an interesting specimen rather than a human being. She had given up hope early on that the doctors would cure me. *All they'd do is put him through weird experiments or give him untested medicines, observe his reactions, and show off their findings at a conference*, she wrote in her diary. And so Mom, like so many other overprotective mothers, made a declaration that was both unconvincing and clichéd.

"I know what's best for my child."

On my last day at the hospital, Mom spat on a flower bush in front of the hospital building and said, "Those hacks don't even know what's in their own goddamned brains."

She could be so full of swagger sometimes.

7

Mom blamed stress during her pregnancy, or the one or two cigarettes she had smoked in secret, or the few sips of beer she couldn't resist in the last month before her due date, but it was obvious to me why my brain was messed up. I was just unlucky. Luck plays a huge part in all the unfairness of the world. Even more than you'd expect.

Things being the way they were, Mom may have hoped that I would at least have a large computer-level memory like in the movies, or some extraordinary artistic talent in my drawings— something to offset my lack of emotions. If so, I could've been on TV, and my sloppy paintings would've sold for more than ten million *won*. Unfortunately, I was no genius.

After the Mickey Mouse Hairband Incident, Mom began "educating" me in earnest. On top of its tragedy and misfortune, the fact that I didn't feel much basically implied serious dangers ahead.

No matter how much people scolded me with their angry looks, it didn't work. Screaming, yelling, raising eyebrows . . . I couldn't grasp that all these things meant something specific, that there was an implication behind each action. I just took things at face value.

Mom wrote down a few sentences on colored paper and pasted them onto a larger piece of paper. She put them all over the walls.

When cars come too close to you → Dodge or run away.
When people come too close to you → Make way so that you don't bump into them.
When others smile → Smile back.

At the bottom, it said:

Note: For expressions, try to mirror the expression the other person makes.

It was a little too much for seven-year-old me to grasp.

The examples on the paper got longer and longer. While other kids were memorizing multiplication tables, I was memorizing these examples like studying the chronology of the ancient dynasties. I tried to match each item to the appropriate, corresponding reaction. Mom tested me regularly. I committed to memory each "instinctive" rule that other kids had no problem picking up. Granny tutted that this kind of cramming was pointless, but she still cut out the arrow shapes to glue onto the paper. The arrows were her job.

8

Over the next few years, my head grew bigger, but my almonds stayed the same. The more complex relationships got, the more diversions I encountered that hadn't been covered by Mom's equations, and the more that happened, the more I became a target. By the first day of the new school year, I had already been marked as the weird kid. I was called out to the playground and made fun of in front of everyone. Kids often asked me strange questions, and I answered straightforwardly, not knowing how to lie or why they were laughing so hard. Without meaning to, I stabbed a dagger into Mom's heart every day.

But she never gave up.

"Don't stand out. That's all you need to do."

Which meant I couldn't let them find out that I was different. If I did, I would stand out, which would make me a target. But learning rules as basic as move-aside-when-a-car-closes-in was no longer enough. It was now time to master exceptional acting skills to hide my abnormality. Mom was like a playwright and never tired of using her imagination to come up with different situations. Now I needed to read the true meanings behind words, as well as memorize the proper intentions behind my responses.

For example, when kids showed me their new school supplies or toys and explained what they were, Mom said what they were really doing was "bragging."

According to her, the correct answer was: "That's awesome," which implied "envy."

When someone said positive things like I was handsome or I did a good job (of course, I had to memorize separately what "positive" statements were), I should respond as follows: "Thank you," or "It's nothing."

Mom said "Thank you" was the sensible answer and "It's nothing" was more laid-back, which could make me look much cooler. Of course, I always chose the simpler answers.

9

Because of her poor handwriting, Mom printed out each *hanja* for happiness, anger, sadness, joy, love, hatred, and desire from the Internet on letter-size paper, one big character at a time. With a tsk-tsk sound, Granny scolded Mom that everything should be done with effort and care. Then she traced those letters big as if she were drawing pictures, even though she couldn't read *hanja* at all. Mom took the letters from Granny and pasted them all over the house like family creeds or talismans.

Whenever I put on my shoes, the character for happiness smiled at me from above the shoe rack, and every time I opened the fridge, I had to see the character "love." At bedtime, "joy" would look down at me from the head of the bed. The words were randomly placed around the house, but Mom superstitiously made sure the negative characters, such as the ones for anger, sadness, and hatred, were all pasted on the bathroom walls. As time passed and with damp bathroom air, the paper creased and the negative letters faded. So Granny would rewrite them regularly, eventually learning them by heart and polishing them in stylish calligraphy.

Mom also created a "human emotion game" where she would suggest a situation, and I'd have to guess what the related emotion should be. It went something like this: *What are the correct emotions when someone gives you tasty food?* The answers were "happiness" and "gratitude." *What are you supposed to feel when someone hurts you?* The answer was "anger."

One time I asked Mom what I should feel when somebody gave me bad food. The question caught her by surprise. She puzzled over it for a long time and responded that at first, I could feel "angry" at the bad taste (I remembered a couple times when Mom criticized a restaurant for its awful taste). But she said people could still feel "happy" or "grateful," depending on their personality. (I also remembered that every time Mom complained, Granny would scold Mom to just appreciate having food at all).

By the time my age hit double digits, there were more instances when Mom needed time to tell me how I should react or when her answers were vague. As if to suspend all additional questions, she told me to just memorize the basic concepts of the main emotions.

"You don't need to get into the details, just nail the basics. At least it'll make you seem like a 'normal person,' even if you might seem cold."

To be honest, I couldn't have cared less. Whether I was normal or not made little to no difference. To me, it was as subtle as the differences in the nuance of the words.

10

Thanks to Mom's persistent efforts and my mandatory daily training, I slowly learned to get along at school without too much trouble. By the time I was in fourth grade, I had managed to blend in, making Mom's dream come true. Most of the time, it was enough to stay silent. I had discovered that if I kept quiet when I was expected to get angry, it made me look patient. If I kept silent when I was supposed to laugh, it made me look more serious. And if I kept silent when I was expected to cry, it made me look strong. Silence was definitely golden. I still habitually said, "Thank you" and "I'm sorry." They were the magic words that helped me get through most tricky situations. That was the easy part. As easy as being handed a thousand *won* and giving back a couple hundred *won* in change.

The hard part was when I had to hand someone a thousand *won* first. That is, to express what I wanted and what I liked. It was hard because to do it, I'd need extra energy. It was like paying first when there was nothing I wanted to buy and when I had no idea what anything cost. It was as overwhelming as trying to make big waves on a serene lake.

For example, if I happened to look at a Choco-Pie I didn't actually want, I had to force myself to say, "That looks good."

And then ask, "Can I have one?" with a smile. Or, if somebody bumped into me or broke a promise, I had to shoot back, "How could you do this to me!" Then cry and clench my fists.

Those were the hardest tasks for me. I would rather not have been involved in them at all. But if I seemed too calm, like a serene lake, Mom said I could also be labeled as a weirdo. She added that I should act out these emotions once in a while.

"Human beings are a product of their education, after all. You can do it."

Mom said everything was for my sake, calling it *love*. But to me, it seemed more like we were doing this out of her own desperation not to have a child that was different. Love, according to Mom's actions, was nothing more than nagging about every little thing, with teary eyes, about how one should act *such and such in this and that situation*. If that was love, I'd rather neither give nor receive any. But of course, I didn't say that out loud. That was all thanks to one of Mom's codes of conduct—*Too much honesty hurts others*—which I had memorized over and over so that it was stuck in my brain.

11

To use Granny's own words, I was more "on the same wavelength" with her than with Mom. Actually, Mom and Granny didn't share any similar physical or personality traits. They didn't even like the same things—aside from the fact they both loved plum-flavored candy.

Granny said that when Mom was little, the first thing Mom ever stole at a store was a piece of plum-flavored candy. Right after Granny said, "The first," Mom quickly shouted, "and the last!" and Granny simply added with a chuckle, "Good thing she stopped at stealing candy."

The two had a special reason for loving the plum candy. *Because it has both sweet and blood taste.* The candy was white with a mysterious sheen and a red stripe across its surface. Rolling it inside their mouths was one of their precious little joys. The red stripe would often cut their tongues as it melted away first.

"I know this sounds funny, but the salty blood taste actually goes well with the sweetness," Granny would say with a wide smile, a bag of plum candies in her arms, while Mom looked for ointment. It's strange, but I was never bored with anything Granny said, no matter how many times I heard her say it.

———————

Granny came into my life out of nowhere. Before Mom became tired of life on her own and reached out for help, they hadn't talked for nearly seven years. Their sole reason for cutting family ties was because of someone not in the family, who later became my dad.

Granny lost Grandpa to cancer when she was pregnant with Mom. From then on, she had dedicated her life to making sure her daughter wouldn't be picked on for being a fatherless child. She basically sacrificed herself for Mom. Fortunately, Mom— though not exceptional—did pretty well in school and made it to one of the women's universities in Seoul. All these years Granny had worked hard to raise her precious child, only to have her fall for some punk (that's what she called Dad) who sold accessories at a street stall in front of her college. The punk declared his eternal love to Mom, putting a ring (quite possibly from his cheap accessory stand) on her finger. Granny vowed that the marriage would take place over her dead body, to which Mom retorted that love is not for some nobody to sign off on for approval. Mom got a slap on the cheek as a result.

"If you disapprove so much I might as well get pregnant!" Mom threatened. Exactly one month after, she made good on that threat. "If you have the baby, you'll never see me again." Granny gave Mom an ultimatum, and Mom left home, making it real. That was how they cut their ties, or so they thought.

I've never seen Dad in person. I've only seen him in photos a few times. When I was still in my mom's womb, a drunk motorbike rider crashed into Dad's accessories stand. Dad died instantly, leaving behind his cheap, colorful accessories. It became even more difficult for Mom to reach out to Granny. After leaving for love, she didn't want to come back bringing all her misfortune into the house. And so seven years passed. During those years, Mom tried to get by and held out until she realized all this enduring was no use. Until the very brink of a breakdown. Until she finally realized she couldn't bear it—bear me—on her own anymore.

12

Granny and I first met at McDonald's. It was a strange day. Mom ordered two burger combos, something she rarely bought, but she didn't touch a thing. Her gaze was fixed on the door, and whenever someone came in, she kept sitting up straight then slouching, her eyes widening then narrowing. When I later asked her what that was, Mom said that was one of the ways your body reacts when you are both afraid and relieved at the same time.

Finally, when Mom got tired of waiting and had stood up to leave, the door swung open and the wind rushed in. There stood a big woman with broad shoulders. On her gray hair she had a purple hat with a feather. She looked like Robin Hood from one of those children's books. That woman was my mom's mom.

Granny was very big. There were no other words to accurately describe her. If I had to try, I would say that she was like a huge, everlasting oak tree. Her body, voice, even her shadow was enormous. Her hands especially were thick like those of a strong-man. She sat in front of me, folded her arms, and pressed her lips tight. Mom lowered her eyes and mumbled to say something, but Granny stopped her with a low, thick voice.

"Eat first."

Reluctantly, Mom started stuffing the cold burger into her mouth. There was a long silence between them even after Mom ate her last french fry. I licked my fingers to pick up and eat the crumbs on the plastic tray, one by one, waiting for their next move.

Mom bit her lips and just looked down at her shoes in front of Granny's firm folded arms. When there was literally nothing left on the tray, Mom finally worked up the courage to put her hands on my shoulders and say in a tiny, faint voice, "This is him."

Granny took a deep breath, leaned back in her chair, and grunted. Later, I asked Granny what that sound had meant. She said it meant something like, "You could've had a better life, poor wench."

"You're a mess!" Granny shouted, so loud that her voice echoed throughout the whole place.

People looked at us as Mom started to weep. Between her barely open lips, she poured out to Granny everything she had gone through in the past seven years. To me, it merely sounded like a series of sobbings and snifflings and the occasional blowing of her nose, but Granny managed to understand everything Mom said. Granny's locked arms were released, her hands resting on her knees, the glow on her face now gone. While Mom was describing me, Granny's face had even looked rather similar to Mom's. After Mom finished talking, Granny remained silent for a while. Then her face suddenly changed.

"If what your mom says is true, you're surely a monster."

Mom gaped at Granny, who had now drawn her face close to mine, smiling. The corners of her mouth turned up at the edges while the outer corners of her eyes drooped. It was as if her eyes and mouth were about to meet.

"And the most adorable little monster you are!"

She stroked my head so much it hurt. That was how our life together began.

13

After moving in with Granny, Mom opened a used-book store. Of course it was only possible with Granny's help. But Granny, who Mom always said loved to hold a grudge, grumbled at every opportunity.

"I sold *tteokbokki* spicy rice cakes my whole life to pay for my only child's education, but look at you, selling old books away instead of studying books. Way to go, you *rotten wench*."

Taken literally, *rotten wench* had an awful meaning, but even still, Granny showered Mom with it day and night.

"What kind of mother calls her daughter a rotten wench, huh?"

"What's wrong with that? Everybody will eventually rot to death. I'm not cussing, just telling the truth."

Anyway, as we reunited with Granny, we were able to end the never-ending cycle of moving in and out, and finally settled in for good. At least Granny didn't nag at Mom to get another job that paid more. Granny had an admiration for letters. That's why she used to buy Mom many books despite being pressed for cash, and had hoped her daughter would grow up into a well-read, well-educated woman. In fact, Granny had wanted Mom to become a writer. Specifically, she had wanted her to be an "unmarried woman of words" who spent her entire life in solitude yet aged gracefully. That was the kind of life Granny would have wanted for herself, if only she could turn back the clock. It was part of the reason she gave Mom the name Jieun, which meant "author."

"Whenever I called her, *Jieun, Jieun*, I thought fancy words would flow from the tip of her pen. I had her read as many books as possible, hoping she'd become an intellectual. Who knew the only thing she'd learn from books was to fall head over heels in love with some ignorant punk. *Aigoo* . . ." Granny often complained.

Because there already was a vibrant online market for used goods, no one thought that running a used-book store offline would make any money. But Mom was determined. A used-book store was the most impractical decision my practical mom had ever made. It had been a cherished dream of hers for many years. There had even been a time in her life when she had also dreamed of becoming a writer as Granny wished. But Mom said she dared not write about all the scars life had left her over the years. Writing would mean she'd have to sell her own life, and she didn't have the confidence to do that. Basically, she didn't have the guts to be a writer. Instead, she decided to sell books by other writers. Books that were already drenched in the scent of time. Not new ones that would regularly flow into the bookstores, but ones that Mom could handpick volume by volume. Hence, used books.

The store was in an alley in a residential area in Suyu-dong, a quiet neighborhood that many people still call by its old name Suyu-ri. I doubted anybody would come all the way here to get used books, but Mom was confident. She had a knack for picking out old niche books that readers would love, plus she bought them at cheap prices. Our house was connected to the back of the store: two bedrooms, one living room, and a bathroom without a tub. Just enough for the three of us. We stepped out from our bedrooms to greet customers and when we felt lazy we just closed the store. The words "Used-Book Store" went up on the sparkling glass window, as did a sign that read "Jieun's Bookstore." The night before our opening day, Mom dusted off her hands and smiled.

"No more moving. This is our home."

That became true. Granny often mumbled to herself in disbelief, because to her surprise, we managed to sell just enough books to afford our living expenses.

14

I also felt comfortable at our bookstore-home. Other people might say they "like" it or even "love" it, but in my vocabulary, "comfortable" was the best scale. To be more specific, I felt connected to the smell of old books. The first time I smelled them, it was as if I'd encountered something I already knew. I would flip open the books and smell them whenever I could, while Granny nagged me, asking what the point of smelling musty books was.

Books took me to places I could never go otherwise. They shared the confessions of people I'd never met and lives I'd never witnessed. The emotions I could never feel, and the events I hadn't experienced could all be found in those volumes. They were completely different by nature from TV shows or movies.

The worlds of movies, soap operas, or cartoons were already so meticulous that there were no blanks left for me to fill in. These stories on screen existed exactly as they had been filmed and drawn. For example, if a book had the description, "A blond lady sits cross-legged on a brown cushion in a hexagon-shaped house," a visual adaptation would have everything else decided as well, from her skin tone and expression to even the length of her fingernails. There was nothing left for me to change in that world.

But books were different. They had lots of blanks. Blanks

between words and even between lines. I could squeeze myself in there and sit, or walk, or scribble down my thoughts. It didn't matter if I had no idea what the words meant. Turning the pages was half the battle.

> I shall love thee.
> Even if I can never know whether my love would be a sin or poison or honey, I shall not stop this journey of loving thee.

The words didn't speak to me at all, but it didn't matter. It was enough that my eyes moved along the words. I smelled the books, my eyes slowly tracing the shape and strokes of each letter. To me, that was as sacred as eating almonds. Once I'd felt around a letter long enough with my eyes, I read it out loud. *I, shall, love, thee. Even if, I can, neverknow, whethermy, love-would, be-a, sinor, poison-or, honey-I, shallnot, stopthisjour-, neyof, lov,-ingthee.*

I'd chew on the letters, savor them, and spit them out with my voice. I'd do this again and again until I memorized all of them. Once you repeat the same word over and over, there comes a time when its meaning fades. Then at some point, letters go beyond letters, and words beyond words. They start to sound like a meaningless, alien language. That's when I actually feel those incomprehensible words like "love" or "eternity" start speaking to me. I told Mom about this fun game.

"Anything will lose its meaning if you repeat it often enough," she said. "At first you feel you are getting the hang of it, but then as time goes by, you feel like the meaning's changing and becoming tarnished. Then, finally, it gets lost. Completely fades to white."

Love, Love, Love, Love, Love, Lo, ve, Looo, veee, Love, LoveLo,-veLo,-veLo.

Eternity, Eternity, Eternity, Eter,-nity, Eeeter,-niiity.

Now the meanings were gone. Just like the inside of my head, which had been a blank slate from day one.

15

Time passed through the endless cycle of seasons—spring, summer, fall, winter—and back to spring. Mom and Granny bickered, often laughed out loud, then grew quiet when dusk fell. When the sun painted the sky red, Granny took a swig of *soju* and let out a satisfied *Kyahh*, and Mom chimed in with her throaty, "So good," finishing Granny's sentence.

Mom was popular. She'd had a few more boyfriends even after we'd started living with Granny. Granny said the reason men were after Mom, despite her eccentric personality, was because she looked exactly like Granny herself when she was younger. Mom pouted but conceded, "Yeah, your granny sure was pretty," although no one could verify that statement. I wasn't all that curious about her boyfriends. Her dating life followed the same pattern. It always started with men approaching her and ended with her clinging onto them. Granny said all they wanted from Mom was casual when Mom was looking for father material.

Mom was slim. She wore chestnut-colored eyeliner that made her big, dark, round eyes look even bigger. Her straight seaweed-black hair fell down to her waist, and her lips were always painted red like a vampire's. I sometimes flipped through her old photo albums and found out that she'd looked the same throughout her adolescence until now almost reaching her forties. Her clothes, her hairstyle, even her face all stayed the same. As if she hadn't aged a bit, save for growing taller inch by inch. She didn't like being called *rotten wench* by Granny, so I gave her a new nickname, *unrotting lady*. But she only sulked, saying she didn't like that either.

Granny also didn't seem to age. Her gray hair turned neither blacker nor whiter, and neither her large body nor the amount of alcohol she drank by the bowlful showed signs of decrease as the years went by.

Every winter solstice, we went up to the rooftop, put a camera on the bricks, and took a family photo. Between Mom the Ageless Vampire and Granny the Giant, I was the only one growing and changing.

———

That year. The year when everything happened. It was winter. A few days before the year's first snowfall, I found something strange on Mom's face. I thought short strands of her hair were stuck to her face, so I reached out to take them off. But they weren't her hair. They were wrinkles. I didn't know when they'd appeared, those deep and long lines. That was the first time I realized that Mom was getting old.

"Mom, you have wrinkles."

She beamed at me, which made her wrinkles longer. I tried to picture Mom aging but couldn't. It was hard to believe.

"The only thing left for me now is to grow old," she said, her smile gone for some reason. She stared blankly into the distance, then slowly closed her eyes. What would've gone on in her mind? Was she imagining herself laughing like an old grandma in her golden years?

But she was wrong. It turned out that she wouldn't have the chance to age.

16

When Granny washed dishes or wiped the floor, she would hum a random tune, adding her own lyrics.

> *Corn in summer, sweet potatoes in winter,*
> *Yummy, sweet, tasty, and sugary.*

Granny used to sell them to passersby at the Express Bus Terminal when she was younger. She would squat somewhere in front of the entrance. The only luxury that young Granny could afford was to roam around the terminal after work. She was especially enchanted by the decorations on Buddha's Birthday and Christmas. Rows of lotus lanterns hung outside the terminal from late spring to early summer, and Christmas ornaments adorned it in winter. It was both her workplace and her wonderland. She said she'd wanted those sloppy lotus lanterns and fake Christmas trees so badly. So when she opened a *tteokbokki* stall with her savings from selling sweet potatoes and steamed corn, the first thing she did was buy pretty lotus lanterns and a miniature Christmas tree. Seasons didn't matter to her. All year round, lotus lanterns and Christmas ornaments hung side by side over her stall.

Even after Granny closed her store and Mom opened the used-book store, one of Granny's ironclad rules was to always celebrate Buddha's Birthday and Christmas.

"No wonder Buddha and Jesus were saints. They made sure to avoid overlapping birthdays for us to enjoy both holidays. But if I had to choose one birthday over the other, my favorite is, of course, Christmas Eve!" said Granny, stroking my hair. Christmas Eve was my birthday.

Every Christmas Eve, we'd eat out to celebrate my birthday. That year, on Christmas Eve, we were getting ready to go out, as usual. It was freezing and damp. The sky was cloudy, and the heavy, moist air seeped into my skin. *Why go through all the hassle, it's just a birthday*, I thought to myself, buttoning up my coat. And I really meant it. We shouldn't have gone out that day.

17

The city was full of crowds. The only difference from other Christmas Eves was that it began to snow right after we got on the bus. There was an endless traffic jam as a radio broadcaster reported that the heavy snowfall would continue the next day, marking the first white Christmas in a decade. As long as I could remember, I'd never had snow on my birthday until that year.

The snow piled up fearfully fast as if it meant to devour the whole city. The once gray city now looked much softer. Maybe because of the view, people on the bus didn't seem too annoyed by the traffic. Mesmerized, they stared out the window and took pictures with their cell phones.

"I want *naengmyeon*," said Granny.

"And hot pork *mandu*," Mom followed, smacking her lips.

"And hot soup," I chimed in. They looked at each other and giggled. It must've reminded them of the other day when I had asked why people rarely ate *naengmyeon* in winter. They probably thought I craved it.

After dozing off on the bus, we got off and walked along Cheonggyecheon stream endlessly. It was a white world. I looked up to see snowflakes rushing down. Mom yelled and stuck her tongue out to taste the snow like a child.

It turned out that the restaurant with a long tradition where Granny had been was no longer there in the corner of the alley-way. By the time the moisture that soaked the hems of our pants crept up and felt cold against our calves, we had finally found another store that Mom had just looked up on her cell phone. It was a franchise restaurant surrounded by rows of coffee shops.

The words "Pyongyang-style *Naengmyeon*" were on the wall in big letters, and as if to prove it, the cold noodles were so soggy that they broke into pieces as soon as they touched my teeth, and that was not even the worst part. The soup was stale, the big *mandus* were burned, and the *naengmyeon* broth tasted like Sprite. Even someone who had *naengmyeon* for the first time would know it was bad and sloppy. Despite that, Mom and Granny devoured and emptied their dishes. I guess sometimes ambiance can give you appetite more than the actual taste does. That day it was the snow, of course. Granny and Mom were all smiles that day. I put a huge ice cube inside my mouth and rolled it around with my tongue.

"Happy birthday," Granny said. "Thank you for being my son," Mom added, squeezing my hand. *Happy birthday. Thank you for being my son.* Somewhat clichéd. But there are days when you are supposed to say those things.

We stood up to leave without deciding where to go next. While Granny and Mom were paying, I spotted a plum-flavored candy in a basket on the counter. It was actually an empty candy wrapper someone had left there. A waiter saw me fidgeting with it, smiled, and told me to wait and he would get some more.

Granny and Mom went outside first. The snow was still falling hard, and Mom looked so happy, jumping up and down, trying to catch snowflakes. Granny shook with laughter at the sight of her daughter and turned, beaming, to look at me from the other side of the window. The waiter came back with a large, new candy bag. He tore the seal and out came the candy, filling up the basket like tiny presents.

"I can take this many, right? It's Christmas Eve," I asked, grabbing two fistfuls of candy. The waiter hesitated a little but nodded with a smile.

Outside the window, Mom and Granny were still all smiles. Parading by the two was the long procession of a mixed choir. They wore red Santa hats and red capes and were singing carols. *Noel, Noel, Noel, Noel. Born is the King of Israel.* I stuck my hands in my pockets and felt the prickly edges of the candy wrappers as I walked to the exit.

Just then, several people shouted at once. The singing stopped. The shouts turned into screams. The choir parade was in chaos. People covered their mouths and hurried away.

Out the window, a man was swinging something against the sky. It was a man in a suit that we had seen lurking about before we entered the restaurant. In sharp contrast to his outfit, he held a knife in one hand and a hammer in the other. He wielded both with such force as if he meant to stab every snowflake falling down on him. I saw him approaching the choir as some people hastily took out their cell phones.

The man turned, and his eyes fell on Granny and Mom. He changed course. Granny tried to pull Mom away. But at the next moment, something unbelievable happened before my eyes.

He swung his hammer down on Mom's head. One, two, three, four times.

Mom keeled over, blood spraying across the ground. I pushed the glass door to get outside, but Granny screamed and blocked it with her body. The man dropped the hammer and sliced the air with the knife in his other hand. I pounded on the glass door, but Granny shook her head, barricading it with all her might. She said something to me again and again, half weeping. The man bore down on Granny. She wheeled around to face him and roared. But just that once. Her big back covered my sight. Blood splattered over the glass door. Red. More red. All I could do was watch the glass door turn redder and redder. No one stepped in during that whole time. I saw a couple of riot police, all frozen. Everyone just stood there and watched, as if the man and Mom and Granny were putting on a play. Everyone was the audience. Including me.

18

None of the victims had any relationship to the man. He was later discovered to be a very typical working-class citizen living an ordinary life. He had graduated from a four-year college and worked in the sales department of a small business for fourteen years before he was suddenly laid off due to the recession. He had opened a fried chicken diner with his severance pay but had to close it in less than two years. In the meantime, he fell into debt, and his family left him. He shut himself in his house afterward, for three and a half long years. He never left his semi-basement room aside from grocery shopping at a nearby supermarket and visiting the public library every so often.

Most of the books he checked out from the library were introductory manuals about martial arts, self-defense, and wielding a knife. But the books found in his house that he owned were mostly self-help books about rules for success and positive habits. On his shabby desk was a will he wrote in large, crude letters as if he didn't want anyone to miss it.

If I see anyone smiling today, I will take them with me.

His journal contained further traces of his hatred of the world. Many sections implied that he felt an urge to kill whenever he saw people who smiled in this miserable world. As details of his life and background rose to the surface, the public's interest shifted from the crime itself to a sociological analysis of what inevitably drove him to do what he did. Many middle-aged men found his life no different from their own and despaired. The public grew more sympathetic toward the man and began focusing on the realities of Korean society, which had allowed this to happen. No one seemed to care about the victims he had killed.

The incident made the headlines for a while, with titles like "Who Made Him a Murderer?" or "Korea: Where a Smile Will Kill You." Before long, as quickly as foam dissolves, even those subjects were no longer talked about. It took only ten days.

Mom was the only survivor. But they said her brain was in a deep sleep with very little chance of waking, and that even if it did, she would not be the person I knew. Soon after, the victims' families held a joint funeral. Everyone was crying except for me. They all wore the expressions you'd expect, standing before your brutally murdered family members.

A female police officer stopped by the funeral, and as she bowed to the bereaved, she burst into tears and couldn't stop. Later I saw her at the end of a hallway being scolded by an elderly male police officer. *You'll witness this kind of thing every so often, so train yourself to be numb.* Just then, his eyes met mine. He stopped talking. I just bowed at him as if nothing had happened and walked past to the restroom.

I heard people whispering about me for showing no emotion during the three-day-long funeral. They all made different guesses. *He's probably too shocked. What would a teenager*

*know? His mom's good as dead, and he's practically an or-
phan, but it hasn't sunk in yet, that must be why.*

They might've expected visible symptoms of sorrow, loneliness, or frustration from me. But floating inside me were not
emotions, but questions.

*What had Mom and Granny been laughing so gleefully
about?*

Where would we've gone after the naengmyeon *restaurant
if that hadn't happened?*

Why did the man do that?

*Why didn't he break the television or the mirror, instead
of killing people?*

Why did no one step in and help before it was too late?

Why?

Thousands of times a day, I asked myself question after question until I went back to square one and started all over again.
But I had no answer to any of them. I even shared my questions
with some policemen and a therapist, who listened with worried
expressions, who said I could tell them anything. But nobody
could give me answers. Most stayed silent, others tried to answer
but gave up. I knew why. It was because no one had the answers.
Both Granny and the man were dead. Mom would be silent forever. So the answers to my questions were gone forever, too. I
stopped asking my questions out loud.

Mom and Granny were gone, that much was clear. Granny was
gone in both body and soul, and as for Mom, the only bit of her left
was her shell. Now nobody would remember their lives except
me. That was why I had to survive.

After the funeral, exactly eight days after my birthday, a new year came along. I was entirely by myself. All that was left in my life was the piles of books in Mom's bookstore. Everything else was mostly gone. I didn't have to hang up the lotus lanterns and the Christmas decorations, or memorize the emotion charts, or go into town pushing through crowds to eat out on my birthday anymore.

PART TWO

19

I visited the hospital every day. Mom lay still, just breathing. She had been moved from the ICU to a six-bed ward. I stopped by every day and sat next to her, relaxing in the warm sunlight coming through the window.

The doctor plainly said that she had no chance of waking up. That she was merely subsisting and nothing more. The nurse absently emptied the bedpan for Mom. I helped the nurse turn over Mom's body once in a while so she wouldn't have bedsores. It was like I was turning over a big load of luggage.

The doctor asked me to let him know once I decided what to do. When I asked him what he meant, he said he'd meant whether I was going to keep Mom here and pay the hospital bills or move her to a cheaper nursing home in the countryside.

For the time being, I would be able to live off Granny's life insurance. I realized then that Mom had made such preparations in case I was left alone at any time.

I went to register Granny's death at the community service center, where the officers quietly clicked their tongues and looked away. A few days later, a social worker from the center came to see me. She looked at my house and suggested that I move to a youth center, like a shelter or group home. I asked her to give me some time. But it didn't mean I would actually think it over during that time. I just needed time.

20

The house was quiet. All I could hear was the sound of my own breathing. The letters Granny and Mom had pasted on the walls were meaningless decorations now that there was no one to teach me what they meant. It was easy to picture what my life would look like if I moved to a facility. I didn't mind, but what I couldn't picture was Mom, who would be left alone.

I tried to imagine what Mom would say. But she couldn't answer me. I searched for clues in the words she had left me. I remembered what she had said most often, which was to live "normally."

I mindlessly swiped through the apps on my cell phone. An app called Chat with the Phone caught my eye. I tapped it, and a small chatbox containing an emoji popped up.

Hi.

As soon as I hit send, I got a reply:

Hi.

I typed:

How are you?
Good. You?

Me too.

Good.

What does it mean to be "normal"?

To be like others.

A pause. I typed a longer message this time.

What does it mean to be like others? When everyone is different,
who should I follow? What would Mom say?

Come on out, dinner's ready.

The response cut me short, because I didn't even realize I had
hit send. I tried to ask more, but none of the replies were useful.
I wouldn't get any hints from this thing. I closed the app without
typing goodbye.

There was still some time before school started up again. I had
to get used to living on my own by then.

———

I re-opened the bookstore two weeks later. Clouds of dust rose as
I walked along the bookcases. I had customers once in a while.
Some people ordered books online. I was able to buy at a rea-
sonable price a collection of used children's books that Mom had
wanted to buy before the incident. I displayed the collection
where everyone would see it.

It was actually easy to say just a few words a day. I didn't have
to think over or rack my brain to find the appropriate words for a
situation. All I needed to say was yes, no, or hold on. The rest was

scanning bank cards, giving back change, and saying welcome or have a nice day mechanically.

One day a lady who ran a kids' book club in the neighborhood came in. She used to chat with Granny sometimes.

"I see you're helping out during your vacation. Where's your grandma?"

"She's dead."

She gaped at me, then knitted her brows in a heavy frown. "I know kids your age can joke around, but this is simply not acceptable. Your grandma would be so hurt to hear that."

"She's really dead."

"Really?" She raised her voice, folding her arms. "Then tell me, when and how did she die?"

"She was stabbed, on Christmas Eve."

"Oh my god." She covered her mouth. "It's that massacre from the news. Oh mercy . . ." She crossed herself and turned to leave in a hurry. As if to avoid catching something contagious from me.

"Excuse me." I stopped her. "You didn't pay."

She flushed.

After she left, I thought for a while about what Mom would've wanted me to say in that situation. The lady's expression made it clear that I'd done something wrong. But I had no idea what my mistake was or how to undo it. Maybe I should've said Granny was out of town traveling. Actually, no, the lady would've kept asking me questions because she liked to mind everybody's business. Or maybe I shouldn't have taken her money. But then that would've made no sense. I remembered the saying "Silence is golden," and decided to stick to it. *Don't respond to most questions.* But then, what would count as "most" was confusing, too.

A book came to mind, one that Granny, who had rarely read anything except store signs, happened to read and love. *Short Stories of Hyun Jingeon.* I had managed to find the chapbook edition printed in 1986 that sold for 2,500 *won.* Her favorite story from the collection was "Proctor B and the Love Letters."

In the story, Proctor B secretly reads her students' love letters at night, acting out both the boy's and the girl's parts like a one-person play. Three of her female students spot her, and each reacts differently. One sneers at her ridiculous monologue, one trembles with fear at her crazy performance, and one cries with sympathy at her longing for love.

At the time, I told my mom that the story contradicted her lesson, in which there was only one right answer for each situation, but I thought this kind of ending wasn't too bad. It seemed to mean that there was more than one answer to everything. Maybe I didn't need to stick to hard-and-fast rules of dialogue or behavior. Since everyone was different, my "odd reactions" could be normal to some people.

Mom was flustered when I said this to her. She thought for a long time before finally coming up with an answer. She said the third student had the correct reaction because the answer usually came in last and the story ended with her crying.

"But there's also a form of writing that starts with the topic sentence. The first student could be correct."

Mom scratched her head. Not giving in, I asked, "Would you have cried if you saw Proctor B's one-man play?"

"Your mother can sleep through anything," Granny butted in. "She'd be one of the extras playing the sleeping students."

I could almost hear Granny chuckling right next to me.

———

A dark shadow suddenly fell over the book. I looked up to see a familiar middle-aged man standing in front of me. But then he was gone. He'd left a note on the counter. It read, "Come up to the second floor."

21

The bookstore was on the first floor of a low two-story building. On the second floor was a bakery, which was unusual. It had no real name, just a sign that simply read, "Bread." The first time Granny saw the sign, she said, "The bread here doesn't look tasty," though I had no idea how she'd deduced that just by looking at the sign.

The bakery sold only streusel bread, milk bread, and cream bread. It even closed at 4 p.m. on the dot. But still, it was always crowded with people, the line often stretching all the way down to the first floor. Customers at the end of the line would even browse in our bookstore.

Mom used to buy bread there sometimes. The bakery's plastic bag read, "Shim Jaeyoung Bakery." Shim Jaeyoung was the bakery owner, but Mom called him Dr. Shim. After Granny had a bite, she no longer complained about it not looking tasty. For me, it was just okay. It was like any other food.

But this was my first time inside the bakery.

Dr. Shim handed me a piece of cream bread. I took a bite, and thick, canary-yellow cream oozed out. He was in his early fifties, but his snow-white hair made him look almost sixty.

"How does it taste?"

"It tastes . . . like something."

"That's good, better than nothing," he chuckled.

"Do you work here alone?" I asked, looking around. The place had no real interior structure. With a partition dividing an open space in the middle, there was nothing but a counter, a display stand, and a table on one side, and the baking area presumably on the other side.

"Yes, I am the owner and the only employee. It's easier that way. It certainly doesn't need more and it's pretty manageable, too." His answer was longer than necessary.

"And why did you want to see me?"

Dr. Shim poured milk into my cup. "I'm very sorry for what you went through. I've been thinking for a while about how I can help you in some way."

"What kind of help?"

"Well, I know we've just met, but is there anything you need or anything you want to ask?" he said, drumming his fingers on the table, which he'd been doing for a while. His habit, maybe, but it was getting annoying.

"Could you stop making that noise?"

Dr. Shim peered at me over the rim of his glasses and smiled.

"Have you heard of the story of Diogenes? You remind me of him. When Alexander the Great tells Diogenes to ask him for any favor, Diogenes asks the sovereign to move aside because his shadow is blocking the sun."

"You don't remind me of Alexander the Great, though."

This time he burst out laughing. "Your mom talked a lot about you. She said you're special."

Special. I knew what she must've meant. Dr. Shim curled his fingers into a tight ball.

"I can stop the tapping for now, but it's a habit of mine that's a little difficult to quit. Anyway, what I meant was that I was actually hoping I could help with things more . . . regularly."

"Regularly?"

"I could help you financially if you need some support."

"Well, I have insurance money, so I'm good now."

"Your mom often asked me to take care of you in case anything happened. We were quite close, you know. Your mom was the type of person who made everyone around her happy."

I noticed he used the past tense.

"Have you seen her, at the hospital?"

Dr. Shim nodded, the corners of his mouth drooping a little. If he was sad for Mom, it might've made her feel good. That was one of the tips she'd given me. If somebody was sad for my sadness, then I should be happy. The principle that two negatives made a positive.

"Why do people call you Dr. Shim?"

"I was a doctor before, but not anymore."

"What an interesting job transition."

He laughed again. I realized that he always laughed when I said something even when I didn't mean to be funny.

"Do you like books?" he asked.

"Yes. I used to help Mom at the bookstore before."

"Okay, then here's the deal. You continue to work at the bookstore. I'll pay you monthly wages. I own this building, so you can save the insurance money for college or other important affairs and use this part-time job for your living expenses. I'll handle all the complicated stuff if you let me."

I told him I'd think about it, just like I had told the social worker. I had learned to respond to unusual offers by buying time first.

"Let me know if you have any problems. I'm a little surprised that I enjoyed our talk so much. Do your best to sell as many books as you can, might as well do a good job, right?"

"Were you her boyfriend?" I asked him when I was about to leave. His eyes widened, then narrowed.

"Interesting you thought of it that way. We were friends . . . very good friends," he said, his grin slowly fading away.

22

After a few days, I decided to accept Dr. Shim's offer. All in all, his suggestion didn't seem to hurt me. My life went on with no more challenging situations. As Dr. Shim had suggested, I tried to increase sales and spent time every day researching bestselling used books and civil service exam guidebooks that were in good condition and buying copies. Some days when the weather was freezing, not a single customer came and therefore I wouldn't say a single word. When I opened my mouth to drink water, my bad breath assailed my nostrils.

Inside a picture frame on the corner of the table, the three of us remained the same. The smiling mother and daughter, and the emotionless me. Sometimes I would get lost in a meaningless daydream, imagining that they had just gone on a trip somewhere. But I knew their trip would be never-ending. They had been my whole universe. But now that they were gone, I began to learn that there were others in this world. These other people entered my world gradually, one at a time. The first was Dr. Shim. He stopped by the bookstore every now and then, handing me bread or tapping me on the shoulder to say, *Cheer up,* when I didn't really feel down.

When the sun set, I would go see Mom. She just lay still, like

Sleeping Beauty. What would she want me to do? To stay by her side and flip her over every few hours? Probably not. She would want me to go to school. That would be the "normal" life for anyone my age. So I decided to return to school.

The bitter winds slowly lost their force. Lunar New Year came around, then Valentine's Day, and by the time people's coats got thinner, I finally graduated ninth grade and moved from middle school to high school. There were endless complaints on television and radio of how January and February flew by so fast.

Then came March. Kindergarteners became elementary schoolers and elementary schoolers became middle schoolers. I became a high school student. Back to seeing teachers and kids every day.

And slowly, things began to change.

23

The new school was a coed high school that had been around for twenty years. It didn't have a high admission rate to top colleges, but it didn't have a reputation for unruly or delinquent students either.

Dr. Shim offered to come to the entrance ceremony, but I turned him down. I watched the ceremony from afar by myself. It was nothing special. The school building was red outside, and inside it smelled of new paint and new construction materials from the recent renovation. The uniform felt stiff and uncomfortable.

On the second day of the new semester, my homeroom teacher summoned me. She was a chemistry teacher in her second year of teaching. She looked maybe just ten years older than me. As she flopped down on an old purple couch in the counseling room, a dust cloud billowed from the impact. She gave a dry cough into her clenched fist, clearing her throat, *Ahem*, in a small voice. Here, she was a teacher, but at home, she might be the doted-on youngest daughter. Her constant coughing was starting to annoy me when she cheerfully struck up a conversation.

"It must have been difficult for you. Is there anything I can help you with?"

So she had some idea of what I had been through. The psychiatrist and lawyer working for the bereaved must've contacted the school. As soon as she asked me the question, I said I was fine. Her lips stretched thin and her eyebrows raised slightly, as if that wasn't what she had wanted to hear.

———————

Something happened the next day, just before class was dismissed. The homeroom teacher must've put a lot of effort into memorizing the students' names the last couple of days. But no one seemed to be impressed, because the names she had diligently memorized were followed by remarks like "be quiet" or "please sit down." It was clear she didn't have a knack for drawing people's attention. And it must've been a habit of hers to clear her throat because she did that every three seconds.

"Listen up, guys." She raised her voice suddenly. "One of your classmates has been through a tragic incident. He lost his family during the last Christmas holidays. Let's give him a warm round of applause as encouragement. Seon Yunjae, stand up, please."

I did as I was told.

"Cheer up, Yunjae," she said first, holding up her hands high to clap. She reminded me of those floor directors I'd seen on television shows who prompted the audience to cheer from the back of the studio.

The kids' reaction was lukewarm. Most of them only pretended to clap, but a few genuinely cheered, so I heard some applause at least. But the clapping waned quickly, leaving dozens of their eyes fixed on me in complete silence.

It was incorrect to say *I was fine* to her question yesterday. *You can just leave me alone.* That was what I should've said.

24

Rumors about me didn't take long to spread. If I typed "chri" on a search engine, "Christmas murder" and "Christmas crisis" came up as related keywords. News articles about a fifteen-year-old with the family name Seon who lost his mother and grandmother occasionally turned up. They had pictures of me taken at the funeral with my face pixelated, but it was done so poorly that everyone who knew me would recognize it was me.

Every kid reacted differently. Some pointed at me from a distance in the hallway and whispered as I passed. Others sat next to me at the cafeteria and tried to talk to me. I would always meet someone's eyes whenever I turned around in class.

One day, a kid had the guts to ask what everyone was curious about. I was heading back to the classroom after lunch. I saw a small, flickering shadow outside the hallway window. A branch was tapping against the window. At the tip of the branch, tiny forsythia flowers were blooming. I opened the window and pushed the branch in the opposite direction. I thought that way the flower could get some sunlight. Just then, a loud voice echoed in the hallway.

"So what was it like to see your mom die in front of you?"

I turned toward the voice. It was a small kid. A boy who often talked back to the teachers and found it amusing that his actions could stir up the crowd. You see that kind everywhere.

"My mom's not dead. My grandmother is," I responded. The boy quietly exclaimed, *Ohh*. He looked around at the other kids, caught some of their eyes, and they snickered together.

"Oh yeah? I'm sorry. Let me ask you again. How did it feel to see your grandma die in front of you?" he asked. Some of the girls booed, *Hey, that's not funny*.

"What? You guys wanna know too," he said, shrugging and raising his hands. His voice was smaller now.

"You want to know?" I asked, but no one replied. Everyone stood still.

"I felt nothing."

I closed the window and walked into the classroom. The noise returned, but things couldn't go back to the way they had been a minute ago.

25

That incident made me kind of famous. Of course, not in a good way by normal standards. When I walked down the hallway, the crowd parted like the Red Sea. I heard murmurs here and there. *That's him, that boy. Well, he looks normal.* Some of the seniors came all the way to our floor to see me. *That's the boy who was at the murder scene. The boy who saw his family bleeding to death in front of him. But said he felt nothing without batting an eyelash.*

The rumors grew bigger and bigger on their own. Kids who claimed they had gone to elementary school or middle school with me said they had borne witness to my strange behavior. The gossip became outrageous, as gossip often does. According to one rumor, I had an IQ over 200. According to another, I would stab anyone who came near me. One even claimed that it was I who killed Mom and Granny.

Mom used to say that every social community needs a scapegoat. She'd given me all this training because she thought I had a very high possibility of becoming one. Now that Mom and Granny were gone, her prediction turned out to be true. The kids quickly realized that I didn't react to anything they said and started asking me weird questions or more blatantly making fun of me.

Without Mom to come up with sample dialogue for every new scenario, I was utterly helpless.

I was a topic at the teachers' meeting as well. They received calls from parents complaining about how, despite not acting in a visibly strange way, my presence itself was disrupting the class. The teachers didn't quite understand my situation. A few days later, Dr. Shim came to school and had a long meeting with my homeroom teacher. That evening, he and I had dinner at a Chinese restaurant, with *jjajangmyeon* between us. When we almost finished them, Dr. Shim got to the point after beating around the bush for some time, basically suggesting that school might not be the best place for me.

"Are you saying I should quit school?"

He shook his head. "Nobody can tell you to do that. What I mean is, can you put up with all this kind of treatment until you come of age?"

"I don't care. You know that, if Mom has told you about me."

"Your mom wouldn't want you to be treated this way."

"Mom wanted me to live a normal life. Sometimes I get confused what that actually means, though."

"Maybe it means living an ordinary life?"

"Ordinary . . ." I mumbled. To be like others. To be ordinary without having experienced terrible ordeals. To go to school, graduate, and if lucky, go to college and get an okay job and meet a woman I like and get married and have kids . . . things like that. Put differently, to not stand out.

"Parents start out with grand expectations for their kids. But when things don't go as expected, they just want their kids to be ordinary, thinking it's simple. But son, being ordinary is the hardest thing to achieve," he said.

Looking back, Granny must've wanted an ordinary life for Mom, too. But Mom didn't have it. Dr. Shim was right—being ordinary was the trickiest path. Everyone thinks "ordinary" is easy and all, but how many of them would actually fit into the so-called smooth road the word implied? It sure was a lot harder for me, someone who was not born ordinary. That didn't mean I was extraordinary. I was just a strange boy wandering around somewhere in between. So I decided to give it a try. To become ordinary.

"I want to continue school." That was the decision I came to that day. Dr. Shim nodded.

"The problem is *how*. My advice to you is this: remember that the brain grows. The more you use it, the better it becomes. If you use it for bad, you'll grow a bad brain, but if you use it for good, you'll have a good brain. I heard certain parts of your brain are weak. But if you practice, you can make them stronger."

"I *have* been practicing a lot. Like this." I pulled the corners of my mouth upward. But I knew my smile didn't look like other people's smiles.

"Why don't you tell your mom about it?"

"About what?"

"That you're a high school student now, and that you're going to school every day. She would love to hear it."

"That's not necessary. She can't hear anything."

Dr. Shim didn't speak anymore. Of course he couldn't, no one could object to what I had said.

26

Long streaks of rain slid down the window. It was a spring shower. Mom used to love the rain. She said she liked the smell. Now she could no longer hear or smell it. What was so special about the smell anyway? It was probably just the fishy stink of rainwater, rising from the dry asphalt ground.

I sat by Mom's side, holding her hands. Her skin was really rough, so I put some rose-scented moisturizer on her hands and cheeks. I went out and took the elevator to the cafeteria. As it opened, I saw a man standing outside.

He was the man who later introduced me to a monster. Dragging *the boy* into my life.

———

A middle-aged man with silver hair, he was wearing a nice suit, but his shoulders were drooping, his bleak eyes welling up. He could've looked handsome if it weren't for his gloomy expression. His face was dark and gaunt.

His eyes quivered when he saw me. I had a hunch that I would see him again soon. Well, I know "hunch" isn't a word that really fits me. Technically, I never *felt* the hunch.

But on second thought, hunches aren't usually just randomly

felt. The brain subconsciously sorts your daily experiences into conditions or results and keeps a growing record of them. And when faced with a similar situation, you unconsciously guess the outcome based on that data. So a hunch is actually a causal link. Just like when you put fruit into a blender, you know you'll get fruit juice. The way he looked at me gave me that kind of a hunch.

After that, I often bumped into him at the hospital. Whenever I felt someone's gaze on me at the hospital cafeteria or hallway and looked around, it was always him. He looked like he wanted to say something or maybe he was just observing me. So when he stopped by my bookstore, I greeted him like I usually did.

"Hello."

With a slight nod, he went on to carefully browse the bookshelves. His footsteps were heavy. He passed the philosophy section and lingered around the literature section for a while before taking out a book and approaching the counter.

There was a smile on his face, except he didn't look me in the eye. Mom had told me that this meant "anxiety." He asked the price, pushing the book toward me.

"A million *won*, please."

"More expensive than I thought," he said, skimming through the pages back and forth. "Is it worth that much? It's not even the first edition. And it's technically a translation, so it's not like being the first edition would mean much."

The book was *Demian*.

"It's a million *won*."

It was Mom's book. It'd been on her bookshelf since she was in middle school. The book that had inspired her to become a writer. I wasn't going to sell it. What a coincidence for him to pick that, of all the books.

The man took a deep breath. Judging by his stubbly chin, he must not have shaved for days.

"I should introduce myself. My name is Yun Kwonho. I teach business in college. You can search my name online. I'm not bragging, I'm just telling you that I'm a credible person."

"I know your face. We've seen each other a few times at the hospital."

"Thank you for remembering me," he said, his expression softening. "I met your guardian, Dr. Shim, and he shared with me your tragic story. I also heard you're a special boy. Dr. Shim suggested I meet you in person, so here I am. Actually, I'm here to ask you a favor."

"What is it?"

He hesitated. "Where should I start . . ."

"You said you needed a favor. Just tell me what it is."

"You sure are quite straightforward, as I was told." He gave a light smile. "I hear your mom's sick. My wife is sick, too. She will be leaving us soon, maybe in just a couple days . . ."

His back slowly curled like a shrimp's. He paused for a beat and went on. "I have two things to ask. First, I would love for you to come meet my wife. Second . . ." He took another deep breath. "Can you pretend you're our son? It shouldn't be hard. You just need to say a couple things I ask you to."

It was an unusual request. Unusual meant strange. When I asked him why, he stood up and walked around the bookstore. He seemed like he always needed time before saying anything.

"Our son went missing thirteen years ago," he broached it. "We did everything we could to find him but failed. We were well-off. I came back from studying abroad and became a professor at a young age. My wife had a great career too. She and I thought we had a successful life. Until we lost our son. Everything changed afterward. Our marriage was falling apart, and she fell ill. These years have been difficult for me, too. I don't know why I'm telling you all this but . . ."

"So?" I asked, hoping he wouldn't go on for too long.

"And then recently, I got a call that they might have found our son. So I went to see him . . ." He stopped and bit his lips for a beat. "I hope my wife could meet her son before it's too late. I mean, the son she's been dreaming of."

He emphasized the word "dreaming."

"You found your son, who didn't turn out to be what she's dreamed of?"

"That I cannot answer. See, it's hard to explain," he said, his head hanging low.

"Then why me?"

"Would you look at this?" He showed me a piece of paper, a flyer for missing children. There was a photo of a boy around three or four years old, and next to it was a sketch of what he would look like now. I guessed it could be said he looked like me. Not so much that we had similar physical features, but we gave off similar vibes.

"So the son you found didn't look like this?" I asked again because I didn't quite understand.

"Well, he actually did look like this. That means he might look like you, too. But he is not in any condition to meet his mother. Please, I beg you. Would you do me a favor just this once? I could upgrade your mom's room. I can pay for her caregiver, too. I can try to help you with everything I can, if you need anything else."

Tears welled up in his eyes. And as usual, I said I'd think about it.

———

The man wasn't lying. His job, his family, and the tragic story about his missing child were easy to find on the Internet. I remembered what Granny used to say: "It's good to help others if there's no harm." When he came over the next day, I agreed to his offer.

But I would've made a different choice had I met Gon earlier. Because by making this decision, I unintentionally stole something from him forever.

27

The room was decorated with various flowers. Little light bulbs gave off a warm glow here and there. It was nothing like the six-patient ward Mom was in. It looked more like a hotel room from the movies than a hospital room. Mrs. Yun must've loved flowers. Their smell gave me a headache. Even the floral wallpaper was dizzying. I thought we weren't allowed to bring flowers into the hospital, but apparently, there were exceptions.

Professor Yun put his hands on my arms as we walked over to the bed. Mrs. Yun lay there, surrounded by flowers like she was already inside a coffin. I took a closer look at her face. She reminded me of those terminally ill patients from the movies. Even the sunrays from the window weren't enough to lift the gloom over her features. She stretched out her stick-thin arms toward me, her hands touching my cheeks. They felt lifeless.

"It's you, Leesu. My son. My love. After all these years . . ."

Tears streamed down her face. I wondered how she could still manage to cry with such a frail body. As her body heaved, I kept thinking she would turn into ashes and disappear.

"I'm sorry, honey. Mommy wanted to do a lot of things with you, really. I wanted to travel with you, eat with you, and watch you grow by your side . . . Things didn't work out as I'd hoped.

But I'm still grateful to see you've grown up so well. Thank you, my son."

She said "thank you" and "sorry" about a dozen more times before crying again. Then she forced a smile. Throughout the thirty minutes of this whole thing, she kept holding my hands and stroking my cheeks. She seemed to pour all her remaining strength solely onto me.

I didn't talk much. When she stopped talking, and Professor Yun gave me a look, I just said what I had been told to say. That I was raised in a good family with not much trouble, and now I would live with Dad and study hard. So please don't worry. And I gave her a quick smile. She seemed to have tired herself out, as her eyelids began to droop.

"Would you let me hold you for a second?"

Those were her last words to me. Her thin, branch-like arms squeezed me. I felt as if I were caught in a strong trap that I couldn't escape. I heard her heart beating close to mine. It burned. Her arms slid off my back. She's just asleep, said the nurse from nearby.

28

Professor Yun said Mrs. Yun had once been a successful reporter. Vigorous and daring, she wrote witty articles and asked bold questions that caught her interviewees off guard. But there was always a sense of guilt in her heart, as she relied on nannies to raise her own child.

That day, she took off from work for once to take her son to an amusement park. Just the two of them. She went on a merry-go-round, holding her child on her lap. It was a fun outing on a bright, sunny day. Then her phone rang. The child wanted one more ride, but she took him by the hand and led him down. It was a short call. When she hung up and looked around, her boy was nowhere to be seen. She couldn't even remember letting go of his hand.

There weren't as many surveillance cameras back then as there are now, leaving many blind spots. The police investigation went on for a long time but to no avail. The Yuns did everything they could to find their son as their hopes slowly faded. *Please just keep our son alive, and hopefully with a good family*, they prayed, but horrific thoughts would haunt them day and night.

Mrs. Yun constantly blamed herself and realized the success she'd been chasing after was nothing but a mirage. The thought slowly made her sick. Professor Yun also thought she was hugely responsible for losing their son, but being a lonely man, he didn't want to lose her, too. But it'd been a long while since he'd last told his wife their son would return.

A few days before I met Professor Yun, he had gotten a call from a shelter saying they might've found his son. He went there to meet his son for the first time in thirteen years. But the boy he found was nowhere near ready to meet his mom. Because that boy was Gon.

29

Maybe Mrs. Yun had really used all her remaining strength on me. The day I paid her a visit, she went into a coma, and died a few days later. Professor Yun relayed the news in a low, quiet voice. Not many people would be able to share the death of a loved one like he did. Only people like me, whose brain was damaged, or those who had already bid their farewells in their hearts. Professor Yun was the latter.

I had no idea why I'd gone to her funeral. I didn't have to, but I just went. Maybe because she had hugged me so tightly that day. Mrs. Yun's funeral was very different from Granny's. Granny's was an impersonal, joint memorial, with only me standing in front of her portrait. Mrs. Yun's funeral reminded me of a reunion. The guests were all in nice suits. Their job titles and conversations would be described as "sophisticated." I heard them calling each other professor, executive, doctor, and president many times.

Mrs. Yun in the portrait looked completely different. With her red lips, full hair, plump cheeks, and eyes as bright as candlelight, she looked so young. The portrait must've been taken in her thirties. But why would they use this photo?

"This picture was taken before we lost our son. I couldn't find any photo where she was smiling like this from after the incident.

She wanted it this way." Professor Yun said, as if he had noticed my lingering question.

I offered incense and bowed at the funeral altar. She had fulfilled her wish before she died. She met her son. At least that was what she had thought. Would she have been devastated if she had known the truth?

Anyway, my job was done. I was turning to leave when I suddenly felt a rush of cold air quickly spreading throughout the place. Everyone either shut their mouths, as if they had been assailed by a powerful silence, or froze with their mouths open. As if on cue, all eyes swiveled to one direction. The boy was there.

30

The skinny boy stood still, his fists clenched tight. His arms and legs were much longer than his short, stocky body, a bit like Joe's from the cartoon *Tomorrow's Joe*. But the boy's body wasn't the kind toned from frequent exercise. It was more like the body of third-world children I'd seen in a documentary. The kind trained for survival, rummaging in trash bins and begging tourists for a dollar. His dark skin had no luster. Below his eyebrows, as dark as shadows, his eyes glinted like black pebbles, glaring at everyone. It was his eyes that silenced the room. He was like a wild beast killing his own cub first and baring his teeth at people who had no intention to harm.

He spat on the floor. Like spitting was his way of greeting. He'd done it before, when I had first met him. In fact, the funeral was my second time meeting him.

A few days earlier, a new student had come to our class. The homeroom teacher slid open the classroom door, revealing a skinny boy standing behind her. He folded his arms and leaned on one foot, a sign that showed he wasn't intimidated at all in front of complete strangers. The teacher staggered and babbled rather, as if she were the transfer student, then asked Gon to introduce himself.

"Can *you* just do it for me?" he said, shifting his weight to his other foot.

The kids burst into laughter. Some of them cheered, clapping and roaring. The teacher flapped her hands at her flushed face.

"This is Yun Leesu. Now, why don't you say hi to your class-mates."

"Well . . ." Gon cracked his neck and pushed his tongue into one cheek, then the other. He smirked, turned his head sideways, and spat.

"Done."

Everyone cheered louder. But some cursed, in which case the teacher would normally give a warning or take them to the teachers' office. But for some reason, the teacher just turned her head, silent. Her face was even more flushed now, from trying to swallow the words she wanted to spit out. An hour after Gon's introduction, he left school early.

Kids started tracking down Gon's background, and in a mere thirty minutes, the whole class knew what kind of life Gon had been through.

One kid told us what he had heard from his cousin. Gon had attended the cousin's school right before ours, after he'd served a term at a juvenile detention center. The kid made a call to his cousin. At everyone's request, the call was put on speakerphone. Kids surrounded him with a sense of solidarity that hadn't been seen in months. Some stood on the desk to hear better. I was sitting far away, but I heard this much clearly:

"That dude is a total gangster. He must've done everything except murder someone."

Someone teased me, "Too bad for you, retard. Your days are gone now."

When Gon slid open the classroom door the next day, everyone went dead silent. He swaggered along to his desk without a word. Kids either avoided his eyes or buried their heads in their textbooks. Gon broke the silence, flinging down his backpack.

"Who was it?" It seemed he somehow became aware of the gossip from yesterday. "Who the fuck ratted me out? Speak up before it's too late."

The very air quivered. Our primary source stood up, trembling.

"I, I just . . . m-my cousin said he knew you . . ." His voice dissolved.

Gon pushed out his cheek with his tongue as if it's a habit of his. "Thanks. Now I don't need to introduce myself. That's who I am." Gon plopped down in his chair.

The day I heard about Mrs. Yun's death, Gon was absent from school. They said one of his family members passed away. Even then, it didn't hit me. That Gon was the boy. That *he* was the real son of Mrs. Yun, who had mistaken me as her dream son.

31

Gon passed through the crowd to bow before the funeral portrait of his mom. Nothing in particular happened. He followed after his father to burn incense, place a glass full of *soju* on the counter, and bow again. All his gestures were so quick and he bowed only once before standing up with a curt nod. Professor Yun gently nudged Gon's back, suggesting Gon was supposed to bow once more. But Gon shrugged him off and disappeared.

Professor Yun asked me to sit down and eat before I left. The food was similar to Mom's holiday dishes—hot *yukgaejang*, *jeon*, *kkultteok*, and fruit. I hadn't noticed I was starving until I found myself gobbling it all down.

People don't realize how loud they can be when they gossip. Even when they try to whisper, the gossip always goes straight into others' ears. Throughout the entire meal, stories about Gon floated in the air. That he'd come two days late because he refused to come, that he'd gotten into trouble the moment he was released from the center, that his school transfers cost however much, that another boy was pretending to be their son. All these stories gave me a headache. I just sat in the corner quietly, my back to them. I didn't know why, but somehow, I felt I had to stay.

As night fell and most of the visitors left, Gon returned. He walked toward me, staring daggers at me as if he was singling me out with his eyes. He sat at my table, his eyes still fixed on me. He slurped two bowls of *yukgaejang* at once without a word before he wiped his face.

"You're the son of a bitch that took my place as their son?"

I didn't have to respond, because he continued, "Brace yourself for some trouble. Who knows, it should be fun." He smirked and left. The next day, it was the real beginning.

32

Gon started to have two guys around him. There was this scrawny one that acted like his assistant, relaying whatever Gon had to say to the others, and the bulky one, whose job was clearly to show off their power. The three of them didn't *really* seem close. It looked like they had teamed up out of an agreement or for some shared goal, rather than friendship.

Anyhow, it was quite obvious that Gon started his new hobby, which was bullying me. He would pop up in front of me out of nowhere, like a jack-in-the-box, wait in front of the cafeteria to punch me, or hide at the end of the hallway to trip me. Each time he executed one of his little schemes, he giggled out loud like he'd received some huge present, while his minions awkwardly laughed along with him like hitting an off beat.

Throughout all this, I didn't react. More and more kids were scared of Gon and took pity on me. But no one told on him to the teacher. Maybe because they were worried they might be his next target, but probably because I showed no sign of needing help. The consensus seemed to be, *Let's just see how it goes for both these weirdos.*

The reaction Gon wanted from me was obvious. There had been kids like him in my elementary school and middle school.

Those who took joy in watching the weak suffer. Those who wanted to see the bullied cry and beg them to stop. They usually got what they wanted through their power. But one thing I knew for sure was that, if Gon wanted to see a change of expression from me, he would never win against me. The more he tried, he would only wear himself out.

———

Not before long, Gon seemed to realize I was no easy match. He continued to rile me, but he seemed no longer as confident as he was before.

"Is he chickening out? He looks totally nervous," kids whispered behind Gon's back. The more I didn't react, and the longer I didn't ask for help, the higher the tension mounted in the classroom.

Gon must've gotten tired of tripping me up or slapping me on the back of my head. Instead, he *announced* that he would have it out with me, once and for all. As soon as the teacher dismissed the class and left, the scrawny lackey ran up to the chalkboard and started scribbling something on it. In crooked letters, he wrote:

AFTER LUNCH. TOMORROW. IN FRONT OF THE
INCINERATOR.

"I've warned you," Gon shouted pompously. "It's up to you now. Don't wanna get beat up? Then don't show up. I will just assume you've chickened out, and I won't bother you anymore. But if you do show up, you'd better brace yourself."

Without responding, I stood up and slung my bag over my shoulders.

Gon hurled a book at me from behind. "You hear me, asshole? I said, get out of my way or I will knock you out!" Gon fumed, his face getting redder from holding back his anger.

"Why do I need to get out of your way? I'm just gonna go about my way as usual. If you're not there, I won't see you. If you are there, I'll see you."

I turned around to leave as he hurled curses at me. All I could think of was that Gon was bullying himself in an exhausting way.

33

By the next day, the whole school had heard about the showdown between Gon and me. The campus was already loud in the morning. The occasional chitchatting hinted at what would follow during lunchtime. Someone said, "Man, time drags." Some other kid said, "There's no way he's gonna show up there, don't you think?" Some kids even bet on who would win. I just focused in class as if nothing was happening. To me, time went by as usual, neither slow nor fast. Then the school bell rang to signal our lunch break.

Nobody sat next to me in the cafeteria, which was normal, until after I finished lunch and stood up to leave. A few kids started following me. As I walked, the group behind me grew bigger and bigger. I walked out the exit door. The shortcut to the classroom involved passing by the incinerator. I plodded on. And there stood Gon. Alone without his minions, he was kicking the trunk of a nearby tree when he stopped at the sight of me. I could see him clenching his fists from afar. As the distance between us was getting shorter, the group behind me scattered one by one like useless dust.

The expression on Gon's face was somewhat conflicted. He was too tight-lipped to look angry, yet his eyes were too upturned to look sad. I had no idea how to read his face.

"He's definitely scared, what a chicken, Yun Leesu!" someone shouted.

Now I was just a couple of steps away from Gon. I kept walking, steady as usual. I would get sleepy after lunch, so my only thought was to take a nap back at the classroom. Before I realized it, I had passed by Gon like he was merely part of the scenery. I heard the kids shout *Wow*, before I felt a light shock in the back of my head. He must've slightly missed me because it didn't hurt. But before I could turn around, a kick knocked me over.

"I said, get, outta, my, fucking, way!" For every word, he gave a kick, ringing my body like a steady ticking of the clock. "You, deserve, it!" The kicks became harder and harder. I was already lying on the ground, moaning, blood oozing inside of my cheek. But I still could never give him what he wanted.

"What the fuck is wrong with you, you asshole!"

He screamed at me, crying almost. The crowd watching us started to mutter. *Hey, he's gonna die, call the teacher!* When a few voices stuck out from the murmuring, Gon turned to them.

"Who was that? Don't talk behind my back, you cowards! Say it to my face. Assholes! Come on!"

Gon grabbed whatever was on the ground and started throwing things at them. An empty can, a wooden stick, an empty glass bottle flew across the air and crashed. The kids ran away, screaming. This was familiar. Granny. Mom. The people on the streets that day. It had to stop. Blood was spilling from my mouth. I spat it out.

"Stop. I can't give you what you want."

"What?" he asked in a huff.

"I have to *act* to give you what you want, and I can't. It's just impossible. So please stop now. Everyone's acting like they're scared of you, but they're actually laughing at you."

Gon looked around. A beat of dead silence, as if time had stopped. Gon's back arched like a hostile cat.

"Fuck, go fuck yourselves!" He started screaming. Every word that came out of his mouth was obscene. Curses, swearwords, and sheer madness that those words couldn't contain.

34

Gon's real name was Leesu. It was his mother who gave him that name. But Gon said he never remembered being called by that name. He didn't like the name because he thought it sounded weak. Out of the many other names he'd had, his favorite was Gon.

Gon's earliest memory was of people who weren't his parents speaking loudly in a strange language. He had no idea why he was there. Noises everywhere. He was with an elderly Chinese couple in a shabby ghetto town in Daerim-dong, where they called him Zhēyáng. For a few years, he never went out of his house. That was why there was no record of his early years.

Then the elderly couple disappeared after a sudden immigration inspection, sending Gon to one foster home after another before he settled at a children's shelter. Because everyone in the town had thought Gon was the elderly couple's grandchild, and there was no official record of the couple leaving for China, they were not able to make further investigations or find his biological parents.

After staying at the shelter for some time, Gon was sent to live with a childless couple. The couple called him Donggu. They weren't well-off and in two years, when their own baby came along, they quickly gave Gon up for adoption. He went back to the shelter, where he got mixed up in some trouble that led him in and out of a youth detention center. It was at the Hope Center shelter that he fashioned the name Gon for himself.

"Do you have *hanja* letters for it?" I asked.

"No, I'm not into that complex shit. I just came up with it." He smiled.

Classic Gon. Out of his many names—Zhēyáng, Donggu, and Leesu—I thought Gon was the most "Gon-like" name too.

The incinerator incident resulted in a weeklong suspension for Gon. Who knows what would've happened if the teacher hadn't arrived just in time. Professor Yun was called in to school to meet with Dr. Shim. Dr. Shim got extremely angry in his low but fervent voice and regretted letting Professor Yun reach out to me in the first place. The school board warned Professor Yun that if Gon's behavior remained the same after the suspension, they would have to transfer him to another school. Professor Yun hung his head.

A few days after, I found myself sitting in front of Gon at a pizzeria. Gon's eyes were no longer glaring. Maybe because Professor Yun sat next to him. I later learned that Professor Yun beat Gon for the first time after hearing about the incinerator incident. Professor Yun was a gentleman, so all he did was hurl a cup he'd been holding at the wall and whip Gon on the calves a few times. But this left a mark on his long-standing self-image as an intellectual, driving him farther apart from his son.

I wonder what it means to get beaten by a father you're re-united with for the first time in a dozen years. Before even having the chance to get to know each other.

According to Dr. Shim, Professor Yun was a man of principle. A man who absolutely hated causing others any trouble, so much so that he couldn't bear his own flesh and blood completely going against his steadfast philosophy. Rather than feeling sorry for his son, he was more angry that the son he'd waited so long for had turned out to be such a *mess*. That was why Professor Yun chose to beat Gon and apologize to others time after time. He apologized to the teachers, to Gon's classmates, and to me.

It was by way of apology that he had arranged this meal with Gon and me at the pizzeria, ordering its most expensive dish. Professor Yun, with his arms stretched, each hand on his knees, said the same thing over and over out loud. As if he wanted Gon to hear it to the core, his voice trembling, his eyes hardly meeting mine.

"I am very sorry to have caused you this. It's all my fault . . ."

I sipped my Coke from a straw, little by little. It didn't seem like he was going to finish talking anytime soon. The longer he talked, the harder Gon's face became. My stomach was growling, and the pizza on the table was getting cold and stale.

"You can stop now. I'm not here for your apology. It's Gon's job to apologize, so maybe you should leave us alone for him to do so."

Professor Yun's eyes widened as if he was surprised. Gon raised his eyes too.

Professor Yun hesitated. "If I take a walk around the corner, are you going to be okay?"

"Yes. I'll call you if anything happens."

Hmf. Gon smirked.

Professor Yun let out a couple of dry coughs and slowly stood up to leave. "I'm sure Leesu feels sorry, Yunjae."

"I'm sure he can speak for himself."

"Very well. Please enjoy the meal. Do call me if something happens."

"I will."

Professor Yun put his hand firmly on Gon's shoulder before leaving the restaurant. Gon didn't react at the moment, but as soon as his father left, he dusted off his shoulder.

35

The Coke bubbled. Gon was blowing into it with his straw, his face turned toward the windowsill. There was nothing much about the view outside, just cars passing by. Then I saw a silver metal pepper shaker in front of the window frame. Its round shape reflected the surroundings like a wide-angle lens. And there I was, in the center. Covered in welts and bruises, my face looked like a boxer who'd just lost a match. Gon was staring at my reflection in the pepper shaker. There, our eyes met.

"You look like shit," he said.

"Thanks to you."

"Do you really think I'd apologize?"

"I don't care."

"Then why did you ask him to leave us alone?"

"Your father talks too much. I just wanted some silence."

Gon snorted as if he were trying to cover his laugh with coughs.

"So, your father beat you?" I didn't have much to say, so I blurted out what had been on my mind. It must've been an inappropriate ice breaker, because Gon's eyes flashed.

"Who told you that?"

"Your father said it himself."

"Shut up, son of a bitch. I don't have a father."

"You can't change the fact that he's your father."

"You want more trouble? I said, shut the fuck up." Gon snatched the pepper shaker. He gripped it so tightly that his fingertips turned white.

"Why, you want to go another round?" I asked.

"Is there a reason I shouldn't?"

"No, I just wanted to ask. Let me know so I can prepare."

Gon seemed to give in, pulling his glass of Coke closer to him. He blew more bubbles into his Coke. I copied him, blowing bubbles into mine. Gon took a bite of pizza, chewed it four times, and swallowed. Then he let out a short, raspy cough. I copied that, too. Chewing on pizza four times, and a cough.

Gon glared at me. He finally noticed me copying him.

"Asshole," he muttered.

"Asshole," I followed.

Gon twitched his lips left and right and saw me do the same. He made a weird face and spat out words like "pizza," "poop," "toilet," "go to hell." I followed him exactly like a clown or parrot. I even matched the number of breaths he took.

As our weird mirror play went on, Gon seemed to be worn out. He stopped laughing, and it took longer for him to come up with difficult expressions or motions. I didn't care and kept copying him, down to the *pfpfpf* sound he made and his subtle eyebrow twitches. My steadfast mimicking seemed to get in the way of his "creative" ideas.

"That's enough."

But I didn't stop. I repeated after him, "That's enough."

"I said, quit it, you asshole."

"I said, quit it, you asshole."

"You think this is funny, bitch?"

"You think this is funny, bitch?"

Gon stopped and started drumming his fingers on the table. When I followed suit, he stopped immediately. Silence, followed by a scowl. Ten. Twenty seconds. A minute. Then he straightened up, and I did too.

"You know what . . ."

"You know what . . ."

"Would you still copy me if I flipped the table and threw all the plates?"

"Would you still copy me if I flipped the table and threw all the plates?"

"I said, would you still copy me if I took a broken plate and stabbed everyone here to death, you motherfucker."

"I said, would you still copy me if I took a broken plate and stabbed everyone here to death, you motherfucker."

"Okay."

"Okay."

"Let's get this straight. *You* started this."

"Let's get this straight. *You* started this."

"If you stop midway, you're a piece of shit, you hear me?"

"If you stop midway, you're a piece of—" But before I could finish the sentence, he swept all the food off the table. He yelled at the crowd, pounding on the table.

"What are you lookin' at, you crazy bitches. Enjoying the meal, are you? Stuff your faces, dipshits!"

He hurled the pizza and all the sauce bottles he could get his hands on in every direction. The pizza landed on the shoe of the woman sitting across our table; sauce splashed over a child's head.

"Why aren't you following me now, you piece of shit! Why you not followin' me!" he yelled at me, fuming. "You started it, what's stopping you now, huh!"

A waiter rushed to stop him, but it was no use. Gon raised his arm as if to hit the waiter. Some customers began taking pictures with their cell phones while another waiter urgently made a call somewhere.

"I said, follow me, you son of a bitch," Gon yelled again, but I was already heading out of the restaurant. I called Professor Yun just like I'd promised. He appeared before the phone rang. He must've been standing by on the nearby street corner in case of any emergency. Professor Yun headed straight in. I watched the mess in the restaurant through the window. Professor Yun's trembling shoulders from the back, his big hand slapping Gon's cheek, over and over and over. His hands gripping Gon's head, shaking it hard. I turned to leave. It wasn't that interesting to keep watching.

———

I was hungry, hardly having eaten the pizza. I stopped by a small snack bar near a subway station and had a bowl of *udon*. Then I headed over to see Mom. She was asleep as always. Her urine tube was dangling out of the bottle from below her bed. Yellow drops of urine were dripping down one by one. I called a nurse to handle it. Mom's face was oily. She would've been shocked to see herself in the mirror. I cleaned her face with a cotton pad soaked with toner and dabbed it with moisturizer.

I walked home. It was a quiet evening. I took out a book with a typical story of a high school dropout returning home. He says he wants to be a catcher and protect children in a rye field. The story ends with him looking at his younger sister, Phoebe, in a blue coat, ride a merry-go-round. I kind of liked the ending that was out of the blue. It was what got me to read it over and over.

Gon's face would sometimes overlap the pages I was reading. His expression when his father grabbed his head. But I couldn't make out what that expression meant.

Just before I fell asleep, I got a call from Professor Yun. He kept pausing, giving way to deep sighs and silence. His point was that he would cover all my medical bills from the incident and that he would make sure Gon would never come near me again.

36

There is no such person who can't be saved. There are only people who give up on trying to save others. It's a quote by the American accused-murderer-turned-writer P. J. Nolan. He was sentenced to death for murdering his stepdaughter. He pleaded his innocence throughout his prison term, during which he wrote a memoir. It later became a bestseller, but he never witnessed it himself—he was executed as planned.

Seventeen years after his execution, the real murderer came forward, and P. J. Nolan was officially proven innocent. The person who had committed the terrible crime against his daughter was his next-door neighbor.

The death of P. J. Nolan was controversial on many levels. While he was innocent of his stepdaughter's murder, he did have a serious criminal history of violence, robbery, and an attempted murder. Many said he was a time bomb, and that even if he'd been acquitted, he would've caused other trouble sooner or later. In any case, while the world judged the now-dead man as they pleased, P. J. Nolan's book sold like hotcakes.

Most of his memoir was an explicit account of his deprived childhood and rage-filled early adulthood. He wrote about what it felt like to stab a person with a knife or rape a woman, and the descriptions were so graphic that some states actually banned the book. He described it as if he were explaining how to organize the groceries in the fridge or put paper neatly into an envelope. *There is no such person who can't be saved. There are only people who give up on trying to save others.* I wondered what might've been in his mind when he wrote these words. Did he mean to reach out for help? Or was it out of deep resentment?

Was the man who had stabbed Mom and Granny a type like P. J. Nolan? Was Gon? Or rather, *was I*?

I wanted to understand the world a little better. To do that, I needed Gon.

37

Dr. Shim was always calm no matter what I said, even when I said things other people would find shocking. He remained composed when I told him what had happened with Gon too. That was the first day I told him about myself in detail. About my naturally small amygdalae, the low reaction levels of my cerebral cortex, and the training Mom had given me. He thanked me for sharing.

"So you must not have been scared when Gon hit you. But you do know that doesn't mean you were brave, right? Let me be clear—I won't stand any more of this from now on. It's also my responsibility. Put plainly, you should have removed yourself from the situation."

I agreed. That was actually all Mom had wanted me to learn. But when there is no coach present, the player slacks off. My brain had simply gone about its business as usual.

"Of course, it's a good thing to be curious about others. I just don't like the fact that the object of your curiosity is Gon."

"Normally, you would tell me not to hang out with Gon, right?"

"Probably. Your mom would have said so. That's for sure."

"I want to know more about Gon. Is that bad?"

"You mean you want to be friends with him?"

"How does friendship work, usually?"

"It means to talk face-to-face, like you and me now. To eat to-gether and share your thoughts. To spend time together with no strings attached. That's what it means to be friends."

"I didn't know I was being friends with you."

"Don't say you're not." He chuckled. "Anyway, this sounds like cliché but you'll eventually meet the people who you're meant to meet, no matter what happens. Time will tell if your relationship with him is meant to be."

"Can I ask why you're not stopping me?"

"I try to stay away from judging people easily. Everyone is dif-ferent. Even more so at your age."

———

Dr. Shim used to be a heart surgeon at a big university hospi-tal. He performed many surgeries, and the results were great. But while he was busy looking at other people's hearts, his wife's heart started to ache. She went speechless, but he still had no time to look after her. One day, they finally went on a trip they'd always longed for. It was a deep island overlooking the blue ocean. Dr. Shim watched the sunset, sipping a glass of white wine. But all he could think about were the things he needed to do when he returned to work. Just before the sun sank into the ocean, he fell asleep. In the middle of the night, he was jolted awake by the sound of a sudden gasp. He saw his wife clutching her chest, her eyes wide. Her heart's electrical signals were go-ing haywire. Without warning, her heart had begun beating five hundred times a minute. Everything happened so fast that all he could do for his wife was to stay by her side, crying, holding her hands tight, telling her to hold on and that everything was going to be okay.

Then her wild, beating heart stopped altogether. There were no electrodes, and no one to rush to his aid when he yelled "Code Blue." Dr. Shim frantically continued pumping her already-still heart like an amateur surgeon. By the time an ambulance came an hour later, her body was cold and stiff. That was how his wife left him forever, and Dr. Shim hadn't held a scalpel since. All he could do now was reflect on how much he had loved her and how little he had showed it to her. He couldn't bear to tear open a person to see a heart beat.

They hadn't had any children, and so Dr. Shim was left alone. When he thought of his wife, he was reminded of the savory aroma of bread. She would always bake for him, and to him the taste of bread was nostalgic. It aroused in him his long-forgotten childhood and brought back faint little snippets of memories. When his wife was alive, there would always be freshly baked bread on the table in the morning. Dr. Shim decided to learn how to bake. He felt that was the least he could do to honor her. Logically, it didn't make much sense. What was the point when his wife was no longer there to eat his bread?

I hadn't known, but Dr. Shim and Mom apparently used to talk quite a lot back then. Mom started out as his tenant and became a regular at his bakery, and they'd strike up random conversations. What Mom had told him most was to take good care of me until

I become an adult, should something happen to her. She rarely opened up to others about me—so much so that she went out of her way to keep my condition a secret. The Mom who shared the details of my life and hers with somebody was not the Mom I knew. It was a relief to hear that she had that somebody.

38

To borrow Granny's description, a bookstore is a place densely populated with tens of thousands of authors, dead or living, residing side by side. But books are quiet. They remain dead silent until somebody flips open a page. Only then do they spill out their stories, calmly and thoroughly, just enough at a time for me to handle.

I heard a rustling among the stacks and looked up to find a skinny boy with a popped shirt collar, hanging back awkwardly before disappearing behind a bookshelf. A star-shaped scab on his head caught my eye. After a while, an adult magazine was tossed onto the counter. A woman with a curly blond mane, big breasts and a black leather jacket that barely contained them, sat on a motorcycle with her back arched and her mouth slightly agape.

"This is such old shit. I'll take this for my antiques collection. How much?"

It was Gon.

"Twenty thousand *won*. Antiques are not cheap, you know."

Gon dug into his pockets, grumbling, and threw out coins and bills. "Hey, you," he said, staring at me with an elbow placed on the counter and his chin propped on his hand.

"You're a robot, I hear. Emotionless, right?" he asked.

"Not entirely."

He sniffed a little. "I did some research on you. More specifi-cally, about your crazy little brain." He tapped his head with his fingertips. It sounded like he was tapping a ripe watermelon. "No wonder. I knew something was off about you. I was going nuts for nothing."

"Your dad told me to call him if you came near me."

"There's no need," Gon snapped, his eyes instantly glinted.

"I should give him a call. I promised."

I picked up the phone but before I brought it to my ear, Gon had snatched it away and flung it to the floor.

"Bitch, are you deaf? I'm saying I'm not gonna bother you." Gon stood up and roamed around the bookstore aimlessly, flip-ping the books for no reason.

Then he asked out loud from a distance, "Did it hurt, I mean, when I hit you?"

"Well, it did hurt."

"So robots do get hurt, huh? That's not a real robot."

"Well . . ." I tried to say something but stopped. It was always hard to describe my condition. Especially now that Mom, who used to help me explain, was gone.

"Well, I do know what it feels like when I'm cold, hot, hungry, or otherwise physically in pain. Otherwise, I wouldn't be alive."

"That's all you can feel?" Gon asked.

"Tickles, too."

"And when you're tickled, you giggle?"

"Possibly. I can't be sure, I haven't gotten tickled in years."

Gon made a deflated balloon sound. I didn't even notice that he was in front of the counter.

"Can I ask you something?"

I shrugged.

"So is it true . . . that your grandma died?" he asked, his eyes avoiding mine.

"Yes."

"And your mom is a vegetable?"

"Technically, yes, if you must put it that way."

"And that happened in front of you? She was stabbed by some lunatic?"

"Right."

"And you just stood there, watching?"

"In retrospect, yes."

Gon's head shot up. He was glaring at me. "What a fucking dumb-ass. How could you just stand there watching your mom and grandma die in front of you? You should've beat the shit out of him."

"I didn't have the time. He died right after."

"Heard about that. But even if he were alive, you would've done nothing. You would've made no difference, you coward."

"Maybe that's true."

He shook his head at my response. "Don't I piss you off, talking like this? Not a change on your face. You don't ever think of them? Your mom and grandma?"

"I do think of them. Often. A lot."

"And you still sleep at night? How can you go to school? You watched your family bleed to death, dammit."

"I don't know. You eventually just move on with your life. I'm sure others would go back to their normal lives too, eating and sleeping and all, although it may take them longer than me. Humans are designed to move on and keep on living, after all."

"What are you, a know-it-all? If I were you, I'd be kept awake every night from the rage. Actually, I couldn't sleep these past few days after I heard what happened. If I were you, I would've killed him with my own hands."

"I'm sorry to cause you insomnia."

"Sorry, you say? Heard you didn't shed a single tear when your grandma died. And you tell me you're sorry? You're a heartless bastard."

"You make a good point. I've been trained to say I'm sorry in proper situations."

He clicked his tongue. "You're beyond me. Crazy dude."

"I'm sure everyone thinks of me that way, although they don't say it out loud. That was what Mom used to say."

"You idiot . . ." He shut his mouth. A beat of silence passed, during which I replayed in my head my earlier conversation with Gon. This time I struck up a conversation.

"By the way, you seem to have a limited vocabulary."

"What?"

"Most of them are swearwords, but they are also limited. Reading books will help you expand your vocabulary. Then you can have better conversations with people."

"So robots give out advice now, do they?" Gon smirked. "I'll take this. I'll stop by again next time I'm bored." Gon shook the magazine he chose and headed out. The breasts of the woman on the motorbike shook too. Gon turned around at the door. "Oh, and don't bother calling that douchebag who claims to be my dad, 'cause I'm headin' home now."

"Yeah, and I hope that's not a lie because I wouldn't be able to tell if it is."

"Acting like a teacher now, huh? Just listen to me."

The door slammed shut, pushing a gust of wind into the store. It carried a subtle scent of summer.

39

The pizzeria didn't report to the school. Professor Yun must've compensated them well. Back at school, that incident only existed in a form of rumor among some gossiping kids. Cold tension was in the air, but after a few days, everyone realized that nothing else was going to happen. Gon kept his head low, not meeting anyone's eyes. His two sidekicks hung out with other groups and came nowhere near him. Eventually, Gon sat eating alone in the corner of the cafeteria and slept through classes instead of glaring at others. It didn't take long for him to be downgraded from a troublemaker to a nobody. As Gon received less and less attention, so did I. The kids' attention was always shifting to weirder, more exciting things. Nowadays, everybody was talking about a girl who'd passed the first round of a televised talent audition.

Officially, according to how the kids grouped us, Gon and I were each other's "enemy." It wasn't a stretch, given our history. So, by unspoken agreement, Gon and I ignored each other at school. We neither talked nor made eye contact. We were just two of the components that made up the school, like pieces of chalk or erasers. No one could be truthful there.

40

"Fuck, this shit's too artistic for my taste. Can't see a thing with those clothes covering everything."

Gon tossed the magazine he had bought earlier down on the counter, muttering to himself. His speech and demeanor were almost the same as before, but somehow weaker. He no longer threw books on the floor, and his voice had lowered by a few decibels. But his posture was more upright, his shoulders straightened.

I had no idea why, but for some reason, I was invaded by Gon's frequent visits—or his raids—against my will. He started to stop by nearly every evening. The duration of his visits was different each time. Sometimes he tossed a couple of meaningless words and took off, sometimes he skimmed through the books quietly or sipped on a canned drink. Maybe his visit was so often because I never asked him anything.

"I'm sorry you didn't like it. But our policy doesn't allow refunds, unless the item was damaged to begin with. And you bought it a while ago."

Pah, Gon said out loud. "I'm not saying I want a refund. I brought it back because I just can't leave it lying around my room, you know? You can keep the money, take it as a rental cost."

"It's vintage, you know. It has hard-core fans, I think."

"Did I just read a classic? Maybe I should add it to my book-list, then."

He chuckled at his own joke. But when he saw I wasn't smiling, he quickly wiped the smile off his face. Laughing along is one of my hardest acts. I could force my lips to twist upward, but that's the best I could do. A kind of smile so forced, that could easily be misunderstood as a mean sneer.

My problem with smiling was what had earned me the reputation of being a coldhearted kid since elementary school. Even Mom had to give up, after tiring herself out from repeatedly explaining the importance of a natural smile in my social life. She proposed different solutions. She suggested that I pretend not to have understood or paid attention. But even if I did that, it was often followed by a long, awkward silence. As for this conversation with Gon, I found it unnecessary to worry about these things. Because we just carried on talking about *classics*.

"It was published in 1995, so it's like the grandfather of magazines. It's a rare issue. Not many people recognize its value, but it's a real classic."

"Then give me another recommendation. Another classic."

"A classic in *that* category?"

"Yes, 'a real classic', as you say."

Such classics are usually kept hidden in a secret place. I led Gon to a bookshelf in the corner. I took out a book from the innermost, dust-filled end of the bookcase. It was a collection of pornographic photos taken at the end of the Josun dynasty. An aristocrat hugging a *kisaeng* in different positions. They were blatant and explicit pictures, some of them actually showing their genitals. The only difference from present-day was that the people in the picture wore *hanbok*.

Gon sat cross-legged in the corner as I handed him the book. Upon turning the first page, his jaw dropped.

"Jeez, our ancestors sure knew what they were doing. I'm proud of them."

"The word 'proud' isn't meant to be used about elders. You really should read more books, you know."

"Bull," Gon said, turning the page. He examined each page thoroughly. He gulped regularly, shrugged his shoulders, and shifted his legs as if his body was tingling. "How much is this?"

"Expensive. Very expensive. It's a special edition, you see. It's actually a reprint of a special edition to be exact, but still valuable."

"Who the heck wants this?"

"Probably people who truly know the value of a classic. This edition is really rare, I won't sell it unless to a real collector. You'd better be careful with it."

Gon closed the book and looked through the other magazines. *Penthouse, Hustler, Playboy, Sunday Seoul.* All rare, valuable issues.

"Who bought all these?"

"Mom."

"Your mom's got good taste." Gon said, then quickly added, "It's a compliment. I mean, she's got some great business skills."

41

Gon was wrong. Mom was everything but a businesswoman. All her decisions—except the ones related to me—were made based on hopeless romanticism and whim. Running a used-book store was the solid evidence. When she first opened the bookstore, she had debated what kind of books she should stock. But nothing special came to mind. So she decided to at least take shape like other used-book stores and stocked technical books, academic books or test-prep books, children's books, and literary books. With whatever money was left over, Mom said she would buy a small espresso machine. Books and the aroma of coffee. They were the perfect combination, at least in Mom's opinion.

"Coffee machine, my ass," Granny snorted. She had a flair for getting on Mom's nerves with only a few words. Mom was furious that her elegant taste was being mocked. Granny didn't bat an eyelid as she said in a low voice, "Just get some smut in here."

Pah, Mom huffed, and Granny started exercising her persuasive skills.

"You know, the best of Gim Hongdo's art was *Chunhwa*, I mean, those obscene paintings. Everything becomes vintage when time passes. The spicier, the pricier! Try finding those," Granny said, and not forgetting to reiterate her original point, "Coffee machine, my ass."

Mom took Granny's advice after mulling it over for a few days. Mom used every means online to get her hands on old dirty magazines and finally managed to make a transaction in person with some stranger at Yongsan Station. Granny and I accompanied her to help carry a heavy load of books. The dealer, a man in his late forties, seemed a bit surprised to see two women and a teenager, but quickly took the money and disappeared with a *poof*. The magazines were bound with a rope, revealing the covers on top. On our way back, people on the subway gave the magazines and us awkward looks.

"Of course they're staring, there's a naked woman tied with a rope." Granny giggled.

"Don't pretend you have nothing to do with this. It was your idea!" Mom shot back.

With more direct dealings, we were able to acquire some rare issues like the classic I showed Gon. After a lot of legwork, we completed Granny's "Classic Collection."

Unfortunately, Granny's prediction had missed the mark. I did see some middle-aged men wandering around the adult magazine section occasionally. But in this day and age, people didn't need to buy erotica in a shop, risking embarrassment like they did in Mom's twenties. There were plenty of other, easier ways to access this kind of entertainment at home and enjoy in their comfort zones. Therefore it would be exceptionally unusual to see anyone purchasing erotic books from a female clerk at a used-book store in the late 2010s. Except for one time when the owner of a used-record store bought some to use as décor, the classics in *that* particular category never sold and were soon tucked away. Gon was the first customer to buy a single issue in broad daylight.

42

That day Gon bought several more magazines for the sake of "collecting" the classics. He asked if he could rent them, and I reiterated that this was a bookstore, not a rental store.

"Okay, okay, asshole. I'm going to return these anyway. You know there's no way I'm keeping them at home."

He sounded much softer, despite the swearword. After a few days, Gon stopped by again, with the magazines. I kept telling him that there was no need for him to return them, but he grunted, "Shut up and just take them."

"Too conservative. No wonder they were published in the old days. Too far from my taste," he added.

I thought it would be pointless to push him further, so I accepted the magazines. I noticed some pages in the middle were missing. A few pages even had holes cut out in the middle. The headline of the magazine survived, dangling, which read, "Brooke Shields." Gon glared at me, self-conscious.

"This was a very rare one. There's hardly any magazines left with pages of Brooke Shields intact, especially in her prime," I said.

"Do you have more of her pictures?"

"Wanna see?" I asked, pointing at a computer on the counter.

I typed "Brooke Shields heyday" into the search engine and clicked the image tab. Hundreds of her pictures popped up. From her early career to her prime. Gon was in awe.

"How on earth can a human look like this." He clicked on her pictures one by one with his mouth agape, but then suddenly jolted. "What the heck is this?"

The picture was titled "Brooke Shields Recent." In her fifties, her wrinkly face filled the whole screen. While her youth may have faded, there was still some faint trace of her beauty. But Gon must've thought differently.

"Whoa, this is really shocking. My fantasies are shattered now. I shouldn't have seen this."

"It's not her fault. No one can stop time, and people go through a lot in life."

"Who doesn't know that? God, you talk like an old fart."

"Should I say I'm sorry?"

"Oh man, why . . . why Brooke . . . what happened to you . . . Dude, why did you show me this. It's all your fault."

That day, Gon vented at Brooke and me alternately, then he left without buying anything.

He came back two days later.

"So I was wondering . . ." he asked.

"What?"

"I've been looking at Brooke's pictures lately. Not the old ones, but the recent ones."

"You came here to tell me that?"

"You're crossing the line lately."

"I didn't mean to, but I'm sorry if you thought of it that way."

"Anyway, I was looking over her pictures, and it got me thinking."

"About what?"

"About destiny and time."

"What a surprise to hear those words from you."

"Sheesh, did you know that even when you say the simplest things, you sound like a dick?"

"I didn't know that."

"Now you know."

"Yes, thanks."

Gon burst out laughing. *Hahahahaha.* I counted five ha's split in one breath. What was so funny about my response? I changed the topic.

"Did you know chimpanzees and gorillas also laugh?"

"Whatever, man."

"And did you know the difference between their laughter and ours?"

"What the heck? If you wanna show off, just go ahead."

"Humans can laugh a lot in one breath, but apes can only laugh a syllable in each breath. Like *ha, ha, ha, ha.*"

"I'm sure they build nice abs," Gon replied with a laugh. More like a snicker this time. Then he inhaled deeply and gave out a long exhalation, *Pheww*, as if to calm his unexpected laugh.

Something was different now. Something had just changed in a moment.

"So, destiny and time. What about them?" I asked. It was strange to have this kind of conversation with Gon but I didn't feel the need to stop.

"I mean . . . it's hard to describe . . . but like, did Brooke know when she was young that she would change? That she would grow old? That she would end up looking completely different from her youth? You know in your head that you'll age and change, but it's like hard to imagine, right? That thought just came to me. Sometimes the people who weird you out, like those homeless people in the subway station muttering to themselves, or those beggars who drag themselves around on their stomachs because their legs are cut off . . . they might've looked completely different when they were younger, you know?"

"Siddhārtha also had similar thoughts and left the palace."

"Sid . . . who? I've heard that name before."

I got tongue-tied. I tried to come up with a response that wouldn't get on his nerves. "Yeah, he's famous."

"Anyway."

My answer must've worked—Gon didn't react much. He gazed into the distance and lowered his voice. "I mean, you and me, maybe someday, we might become people we never imagined we'd be."

"Probably. For better or worse. That's life."

"Just when I thought you were okay, you had to go and sound like a dick again. We've both lived *a* same number of years, you know."

"It's *the* same number of years, not *a*."

"Shut up." Gon pretended to hit me. "Strangely enough, I don't feel like looking at those old magazines anymore. It's no fun. It reminds me of how everything beautiful will fade eventually. Not that a dumb-ass like you would understand."

"If you say you lost interest in Brooke Shields, maybe I can recommend another book that could help you."

"What is it?" he asked nonchalantly.

I suggested *The Art of Loving* by a foreign author.* He looked at the title and wore a strange smile. He brought it back a few days later, telling me to cut the bullshit, but I thought the recommendation still made sense.

---

* The title of the Korean translation is *The Love Technique*.

43

The days were slipping by and it was already early May. The unfamiliarity of a new semester fades away by this time. People say that May is the queen of seasons, but I don't quite agree. The hardest job is transitioning from winter to spring. Frozen ground melting to let sprouts shoot up, colorful flowers blossoming from each dead branch. That's what tough looks like. As for summer, it simply needs to take a couple more steps forward using the momentum of spring. That's why I think May is the laziest of all the months. A month that's overrated. And May was the month that always reminded me I was different from the rest of the world. Everything on the earth glittered, vibrantly. Only me and my bedridden Mom were stiff and gray, like an eternal January.

I was able to open the bookstore only after school, and naturally, sales were slow. I remembered Granny used to say, "If business isn't good, just shut it down." I swept the dust and mopped the floor every day, but for some reason, the space Granny and Mom had left behind seemed to wear down by the day. How much longer would I be able to handle this void?

One day while I was tidying up, I dropped a dozen books I was carrying, cutting my fingertip. It was not something that often happened in a damp used-book store. I just got unlucky because the book happened to be an encyclopedia with thick, hard paper. Absently, I watched the drops of blood dripping down on the floor like sealing wax.

"Dude. You're bleeding."

It was Gon. I hadn't even heard him come in, but he was already next to me. "Doesn't it hurt?" Eyes widened, Gon quickly grabbed a tissue and handed it to me.

"I'm okay."

"Bullshit. If it bleeds, it hurts. Are you really an idiot?" He sounded angry. The cut must've been deeper than I'd thought. The tissue was already soaked red. Gon rolled up another tissue and grabbed my hand. I could feel the pulse from my fingers, beating hard from his tight grip. He put pressure on the cut until the bleeding stopped. "Don't you know how to take care of yourself?" He raised his voice.

"It hurt, but it was manageable."

"You were gushing blood, you call that manageable? You really are a robot, aren't you? That's why you just stood there, huh? Did nothing when your mom and grandma dropped down in front of you. Because you're a robot. You idiot, it didn't even occur to you that they were hurt, that you should've stopped him, that you should've been angry. Because you don't feel anything."

"You're right. The doctors said I was born this way."

Psychopath. That was what kids had called me since elementary school. Mom and Granny would go ballistic over it, but to some extent, I thought they had a point. Maybe I really was a psychopath. I wouldn't feel guilty or confused, even if I hurt or killed somebody. I was born this way.

"Born this way?" Gon said. "That's the shittiest thing people say."

44

A few days later, Gon came to the bookstore holding a clear plastic container. Inside was a butterfly he had somehow gotten his hands on. The box was too small for the butterfly, so it kept banging the sides of the container.

"What is this?"

"Empathy training," Gon said, straight-faced, not even the slightest grin to be seen. So this meant he was serious. He carefully put his hand inside the box and grabbed hold of the butterfly. Its petal-thin wings caught in his hand, struggling helplessly. "How do you think it feels?" Gon asked.

"Like it'll want to move," I said.

Gon took out the butterfly and, holding each wing with each hand, started stretching them out little by little. The butterfly's feelers bent whichever way, its body writhing hard.

"If you're doing this to make me feel anything, you should stop it," I said.

"Why?"

"Because the butterfly looks like it's hurting."

"How do you know? It doesn't hurt you."

"It hurts when someone pulls on your arms. I know it from experience."

Gon didn't stop. The butterfly struggled even harder. Gon was grasping its wings, but he looked away.

"The butterfly *looks* like it's hurting? That's not enough."

"Then?"

"You should *feel* like you're also hurting."

"Why? I'm not the butterfly."

"Okay. Let's keep going until you really feel something."

Gon stretched the wings farther apart, his eyes still looking elsewhere.

"Stop. It's wrong to mess with living things."

"Don't give me some shit you've read in a textbook. I said I'll let go of this if you really feel something."

Just then, one wing ripped. Gon let out a short, sharp breath. The butterfly fluttered its remaining wing in vain, spinning on the spot.

"You don't feel sorry for it?" Gon asked, fuming.

"It looks uncomfortable."

"No, not uncomfortable, I asked if you *feel* sorry, goddammit."

"Cut it out."

"No." Gon hastily reached for something in his pocket. It was a sewing needle. He held it close to the butterfly, which was still spinning on the floor.

"What are you doing?"

"See for yourself."

"Stop."

"Don't you take your eyes off it. Or I'll trash this place. You hear me?"

I didn't want my bookstore to be trashed, and I knew Gon was more than capable of making good on his threats. He stood poised over the butterfly as if he were a high priest before a ritual. In a flash, the needle pierced its body. It struggled in silence, desperately flapping as hard as it could.

Gon glowered at me. Then he gritted his teeth, tearing off the remaining wing. It wasn't me but Gon whose expression had changed. His eyebrows were visibly twitching, and he was biting down hard on his lip, which moments ago had been curled into a sneer.

"How about now? Feel anything? Still just uncomfortable? Is that all you got?" he said, his voice cracking.

"Now I think it hurts, very much. But *you* look uncomfortable."

"Of course, I don't like this kind of stuff. I'd rather kill it in one go, nice and clean. I fucking hate giving slow torture."

"Then why do this. I can't give you what you want anyway."

"Shut up, asshole."

Gon's face was contorted. Just like on the day when he kept stomping me down at the incinerator. He tried to do something more to the butterfly but he couldn't. A wingless butterfly, spinning around with a needle stuck through its body, was no longer a butterfly. The bug was expressing pain with its entire body. Thrashing back and forth, left and right, fighting for its dear life. Was it pleading with us to stop, or trying its very best to survive? It must be pure instinct. Not emotion, but instinct triggered by the senses.

"Fuck it. I quit!"

Thump, thump, thump. Gon hurled the butterfly to the floor and stomped on it with all his might.

45

A small dot was left on the spot where the butterfly had been. I hoped it'd gone to a safer place. And I wished that I could've helped it avoid such discomfort.

I think what happened that day with the butterfly was kind of like a staring contest. A simple game. If you close your eyes first, you lose. I always won in these kinds of games. Other people struggled to keep their eyes open, when I just didn't know how to close my eyes in the first place.

It had been days since Gon last visited me. Why was he angry at me after doing such a thing to the butterfly? Because I didn't react? Because I didn't stop him? Or was he mad at himself for doing what he did? There was only one person I could ask about these questions.

———

Dr. Shim always tried his best to answer my questions. He was also the only one who listened to me talk about my special relationship with Gon without any prejudice.

"Will I live like this my entire life, feeling nothing at all?" I asked after slurping down a bowl of *udon*. Dr. Shim bought me meals occasionally, and he seemed to like noodles. It was either bread or noodles. He swallowed the remaining pickled radish in his mouth and wiped his lips.

"That's a hard question. But I'll say this, the fact that you asked that question in the first place is in itself a big step. So let's keep trying."

"Trying what? You said there was an inherent problem with my brain. Mom fed me almonds every day, but it didn't work."

"Well, instead of eating almonds, I was thinking external stimulation might be worth a try. The human brain is actually dumber than you think it is."

Dr. Shim said if I kept making up emotions, even if they were fake, my brain's little almonds might perceive them as real, which might affect the size or activity of my amygdalae. Then maybe I would be able to read other people's emotions a little easier.

"My brain has been still for the last fifteen years. How can it suddenly change now?"

"Let me give you an example. A person who has no talent for skating will probably not become the best skater even after practicing for months. A tone-deaf person won't ever sing a perfect aria and get applause either. But with practice, you can at least stumble a step forward on the ice or manage to sing a measure of a song. That's what practice can offer—miracles and also limitations."

I slowly nodded. I understood him but I wasn't convinced. Could that work even for me?

"When did you start asking yourself these questions?" he asked.

"A couple days ago."

"Was there a specific reason or incident?"

"Well, no, I was thinking, like I hadn't watched a movie that everybody else had watched. Of course I don't mind, but if I watched that movie, then I'd have a few more things to talk about with people."

"What an improvement! What you just said implies your willingness to communicate with others."

"Maybe it's a puberty thing."

Dr. Shim laughed.

"While you're at it, practice your emotions with something fun. You're basically a blank canvas. Better to fill it up with good things rather than bad things."

"I'll try. I don't know how but it's better to try than do nothing."

"It's not always great when you understand emotions that you were once unaware of. Emotions are tricky business. You'll suddenly see the world in a completely new light. Every little thing around you might feel like sharp weapons. A subtle expression or a few words could sting you. Think of a rock on the street. It doesn't feel anything, and it never gets hurt either. A rock has no idea when people are kicking it. But imagine if it felt how many times it got kicked, stomped on, rolled, and worn down every day, how would it cope? I'm not sure if this makes any sense to you . . . what I'm trying to say is . . ."

"Oh, I understand. Mom used to tell me similar things. Though I know she was just trying to make me feel better. She was a very smart person, you know."

"Most moms are smart." Dr. Shim smiled.

"Can I ask you a question?" I asked after a beat.

"Of course. What do you want to know about?"

"Human relationships? I guess."

Dr. Shim burst into laughter. He drew up his chair and put his arms on the table. First, I told him about the butterfly incident. As my story went on, Dr. Shim clenched his fists. But once I finished, his expression softened.

"So what do you want to know exactly? Why he reacted that way? Or what he must have felt?"

"Well, both, I guess."

Dr. Shim nodded.

"It sounds like Gon wants to be friends with you."

"Friends," I repeated without meaning anything. "Do you tear up a butterfly if you want to become friends?"

"No, of course not," he said, clasping his hands, "but it seems that killing the butterfly in front of you has really hurt his pride."

"Why would he feel his pride was hurt? He's the one who killed it."

Dr. Shim let out a deep sigh. I quickly added, "I know it's not easy to help me understand."

"No, I was actually thinking about how I could put this more simply. So, it's like this. Gon is very interested in you. He wants to get to know you, and he wants to feel what you feel. But after hearing your story, it seems like he was always the one initiating contact between you two. How about you initiate once in a while?"

"How?"

"There are a hundred answers to one question in this world. So it's hard for me to give you a correct answer. And the world is even more of a puzzle at your age, when you have to search for answers yourself. But if you still want my advice, let me answer by asking you this: What did Gon do most often to get close to you?"

"Hit me."

Dr. Shim shrugged. "Sorry, I forgot. Let's leave that one out. What's the next thing he did most often?"

"Uhm . . ." I thought for a while. "He visited me."

Dr. Shim tapped the table and nodded. "It seems you've found one answer."

46

Gon's housekeeper peeled an apple for me while I waited. A plump woman, she had soft eyes and a mouth that made her look like she was smiling even when she wasn't. She managed to peel the apple in one long, unbroken spiral. I sat waiting at a dining table in a stranger's apartment, with the apple before me. By the time the apple turned brown, Gon had arrived. He seemed surprised to see me, but the housekeeper struck up a conversation to make things less awkward.

"Welcome home, Gon. Your friend's here to see you. He's been waiting for half an hour. Your father says he'll be home late. Did you eat?"

"No, I'm fine, thank you," Gon said, wearing an expression I had never seen him wear before. His voice was polite, low and calm. But as soon as she disappeared, Gon was back to his usual, gruff self.

"What're you doing here?"

"Nothing, I just came by to see you."

Gon pouted. The housekeeper brought two bowls of hot noodle soup. He must've been starving actually, since he began to noisily slurp the noodles at once.

"She comes here twice a week. I like her. At least it's more comfortable having her around than that guy who calls himself my dad," Gon muttered. It seemed he still wasn't getting along with his dad. Their apartment was far away from the school. A clean, luxurious penthouse that overlooked the Han River and almost every landmark in Seoul. But Gon said he didn't feel like he was living that high up.

It had been a long time since Gon and his dad last talked. Professor Yun exhausted all his energy in the beginning, trying to connect with Gon, and had soon given up. His classes and seminars gave him a good excuse to spend most of his time outside of the house, and so the gap between father and son remained unbridged.

"That guy . . . never asked me what my life was like before. Or what I'd been through in juvie, or what kind of kids I hung out with. Never asked what I longed for or what made me despair . . . Do you know the first thing he did after we met? He put me into some stuck-up school in Gangnam. I guess he thought I would behave well there, study hard, and go to a good college. But on my first day, I realized it was not the place for a fuckup like me. I didn't belong there. It was written on the faces of every kid and teacher. So I raised hell. Of course the school wasn't having it. They kicked me out after just a few days," he snorted.

"Then that guy somehow managed to transfer me to our school. At least it's a decent humanities school, so he saved face. But basically, all he plans is to pour concrete over my life and construct a new building of his own design. But I'm not that kind of person . . ." Gon stared down at the floor. "I'm not his son. I'm just some junk that came his way by accident. That's why he didn't let me see that woman before she died . . ."

———

Mom. Whenever the word came up, Gon lapsed into a sudden silence. Whether it was mentioned in a book or movie or by a passing pedestrian, Gon would stop talking as if he were mute.

Gon remembered only one thing about his mother: her warm and tender hands. He couldn't picture her face, but he could still remember the moist, soft texture of her hands. He remembered holding those hands to do shadow plays under warm sunlight.

Whenever life pulled brutal pranks on him, Gon would think that life was like having your mom hold your hands one moment, warm and safe, then suddenly drop them with no explanation. No matter how hard he tried to grab hold, he was always abandoned in the end.

"Between you and me, who do you think is more miserable? You, who had and lost a mom, or me, who suddenly met a mom I didn't even remember, only to have her die right after."

I didn't know the answer. Gon lowered his head for a while before he said, "Do you know why I kept coming to see you?"

"No."

"Two reasons. For one, you didn't judge me the way other kids do, thanks to your special brain. Though, it's also thanks to that special brain, I killed a butterfly for nothing. My second reason is . . ." He grinned a little before he continued. "I wanted to ask you something. But fuck, I couldn't bring myself to ask . . ."

There was heavy silence between us. I waited for Gon to speak while the clock ticked. Slowly, he whispered, "What was she like?"

It took me a while to understand his question.

"You've met her. Although only once," he said.

I went back through my memory. A room filled with flowers, her ashen face. I could see Gon's face reflected in hers, though I hadn't known back then.

"She looked like you."

"I saw her pictures but I couldn't see the resemblance," Gon scoffed. But then he asked, "Which part?" He looked straight at me with glaring eyes. I superimposed my memory of her face on his.

"The eyes. The outline of your face. The way you smile. Your eyes drooping at the corners when you smile, making dimples."

"Shit . . ." He looked away. "But she saw you and thought you were me."

"Anybody would do the same in her shoes."

"But she must've tried to find her features in your face."

"What she said to me was meant for you."

"What—what were her last words?"

"She just hugged me. Very tight."

Gon shook his head. Then as if he could hardly get the words out, he whispered, "Was it warm? Her arms . . ."

"Yes, very warm."

His shoulders, which had been hunched and still, gradually sank. His face turned wrinkly like a deflated balloon. His head slowly hanging low, his knees buckled. His body was shaking, his head sunk down against his chest. There was no sound, but I knew he was crying. I looked down at him, saying nothing. I felt like I'd become uselessly taller.

47

We hung out together all throughout summer vacation. On hot summer nights, so humid that my skin got sticky, Gon would lie on a bench in front of the bookstore and tell me stories about himself. But I wonder if there is any point writing down those stories here. Gon had simply lived his life. An abandoned, battered life, one you could almost describe as filthy, for fifteen years. I wanted to tell him that fate was just throwing dice, but I didn't. They were nothing more than some pointless words I'd read in a book.

Gon was the simplest and the most transparent person I'd met in my life. Even a dunce like me could see through his mind. He often said, *We have to be tougher in this tough world.* That was the conclusion that his life had led him to.

We couldn't possibly resemble each other. I was too numb and Gon didn't admit he was vulnerable. He just pretended to be strong.

People said there was no way to understand Gon. I didn't agree with them. It's just that nobody ever tried to see through him.

———

I remember Mom clutching my hand tight when we used to take walks. She never let go of my hand. Sometimes when I tried to wriggle my hand free because she gripped it so hard, she'd shoot me a look, telling me to hold on tight. She said families walk hand in hand. Granny would hold my other hand. I have never been abandoned by anyone. Even though my brain was a mess, what kept my soul whole was the warmth of the hands holding mine on both sides.

48

Every now and then I thought of the songs Mom used to sing to me. She had a bubbly voice when she spoke but her voice turned deep when she sang. It reminded me of the whale humming from a documentary I once saw, or just a breeze of wind or the sound of sea waves from afar. But her voice that once filled my ears was starting to fade. Soon I might forget her voice entirely. Everything I had known was beginning to fade away from me.

PART THREE

49

Dora. Dora was exactly the polar opposite of Gon. If Gon tried to teach me pain, guilt, and agony, Dora taught me flowers and scents, breezes and dreams. They were like songs I heard for the first time. Dora knew how to sing the songs everybody knew, in an entirely different way.

50

A new semester began. The campus looked the same, yet different. Changes were subtle, like the leaves turning darker. But the scent was clearly different. The kids gave off a stronger smell as the season ripened. Summer was pushing hard toward its end. Butterflies slowly disappeared and dead cicadas littered the ground.

As fall came early, something strange happened to me as well. Something hard to describe, something you could hardly call a change. Everything I'd known seemed different, and all the words I spat out with ease wandered awkwardly at the tip of my tongue.

It was on a Sunday afternoon when I was watching a K-pop show on TV. A five-member girl group was giving a speech for topping the charts for the first time since their debut three years earlier. The girls, who looked around my age, were jumping with joy, in short skirts and tops that barely covered their breasts. Trembling, the leader of the group thanked their manager, their boss, their record label's staff and stylists, and their fan club. She rattled off all these names like a rapid fire, so fast as if she'd rehearsed the speech a thousand times over. Finally, she finished with a cliché, delivered half crying.

"Thank you for all your support. What a beautiful night! We love you so much!"

I've seen such speeches countless times, thanks to Mom, who loved watching K-pop music shows. But for some reason, on that particular day, it made me wonder. Can the word "love" be thrown around so casually like that?

I thought of books by Goethe and Shakespeare, whose characters often resorted to death in their desperate search for love. I thought of the people I saw on the news who were obsessed with and even abusive to their loved ones because they thought they weren't loved anymore. I also thought of the stories of people who forgave the unforgivable after hearing just three words: "I love you."

From what I understood, love was an extreme idea. A word that seemed to force something undefinable into the prison of letters. But the word was used so easily, so often. People spoke of love so casually, just to mean the slightest pleasure or thanks.

When I shared these thoughts with Gon, he shrugged them away with a *Pah*. "Are you really asking *me* what love is?"

"I'm not asking you to define the idea. I just want to hear what you think."

"You think I know? I don't know either. That might be the one thing we have in common." Gon giggled before glaring. Changing expressions in a split second was his thing.

"You had your mom and grandma, though. They must've given you plenty of love. Why you askin' me?" he snapped, his voice turning bitter. He ruffled his hair from the back of his neck to the top of his head. "I don't give a damn about love. Not that I would mind experiencing it. The love between man and woman, you know."

He grabbed a pen and started capping and uncapping it repeatedly. The pen went in and out and in and out of the cap.

"*That's* what you do every night," I said.

"Wow, this asshole knows how to make a joke? I'm impressed. But that ain't love between man and woman. It's loving by myself." Gon jokingly hit the back of my head. It didn't hurt. He put his face close to mine.

"Do you even know what love between a man and woman is, kid?"

"I know the purpose."

"Yeah? What is it?" Gon asked, amused.

"Reproduction. It's the selfish gene prompting our instincts to—" Before I could finish my sentence, Gon slapped the back of my head again. This time it hurt.

"You stupid asshole. You know, you're stupid *because* you know too much. Now, listen carefully to what your big bro is about to tell you."

"I'm older. My birthday is before yours."

"Can you cut the jokes?"

"I'm not joking, it's the truth—"

"Shut up, asshole." Laughing, and another flick on the head, which I dodged. "Huh, nice move."

"Can you go back to where you were?" I said.

Gon cleared his throat. "I think love is bullshit, pretending to be all grand and everlasting and everything. It's all a bluff. I'd rather be tough, none of that soft shit."

"Tough?"

"Yeah, tough. Strong. I'd choose to be the one hurting rather than getting hurt. Like Steel Wire."

Steel Wire. Gon had told me about him a couple times before, but I could never get used to the name. I recoiled a little. I felt like I was about to hear things I wished I'd never heard.

"Now, he's strong. I mean very. I want to be like him," Gon said, as something flickered in his eyes.

———————

Anyway, it seemed pointless to expect any real serious answer from Gon. But asking Dr. Shim seemed somehow out of the blue to him.

There was this day when Mom asked a question to Granny, who was carefully writing *hanja* for love, 愛.

"Mom, do you even know what that character means?"

"Of course!" Granny glared at Mom, then in a deep low voice, she said, "Love."

"What does love mean?" Mom asked mischievously.

"To discover beauty."

After Granny wrote the top part of the character 愛, then the middle part, 心 (meaning "heart"), she said, "These three dots are us. This one's mine, this one's yours, this one's his!" Mom's eyes teared up but she turned and went back to the kitchen.

And there it was, the symbol 愛, with the three dots of our family. Back then I had no idea what "discovering beauty" meant.

But, lately, one face did come to mind.

51

Lee Dora. I pictured what I knew of her. An image of her running came to mind. Galloping like a gazelle or a zebra. Actually,
no, those aren't appropriate similes. She was just Dora. Running
Dora. Her silver eyeglasses being tossed on the ground. Her slender arms and legs whipping through the air. The sun glinting on
her glasses. A cloud of dust in her wake. Her fair-skinned fingers
setting the glasses back on her nose as soon as she finished her
race. That's everything I knew about her.

52

On the first day of school, I stood at the back of the auditorium where the boring opening ceremony was taking place. I sneaked out into the hallway when I heard a sound. I turned to see a girl standing at the end of the hallway. She tucked her shoulder-length hair behind her ears, tapping the ground with the tip of her toes. She must've thought no one was looking because she started doing some kind of warm-up. She stretched out her arms and legs and hopped three times before sprinting across the hall-way. Panting, she stopped right in front of me and our eyes met. For five seconds at least. That was Dora.

Her glasses had a thick, matte silver-gray frame with round lenses. The lenses were thin and had so many scratches that reflected the sunlight, making her eyes hard to see.

Dora wasn't like everyone else. She didn't react to every little thing like other kids did. She was calm, so calm that she some-times struck me as a very old woman. It wasn't just that she was smarter or more mature. She was just a little different.

Dora had missed a lot of school that spring. When she did come to school, she often left early without taking any supple-mentary or evening classes. That's why she hadn't seen the inci-dent between Gon and me. In fact, she didn't seem to care what went on around her at all. She always sat in the far corner of the classroom with her earphones in. Someone said she was preparing to transfer to another high school, one with a track team. But she ended up staying at ours. I barely saw her talk from then on. Even in class, she would only stare at the school field outside the window, like a caged leopard.

I did see her without glasses once. It was during the spring Field Day. Dora had been selected as our class representative in the 200-meter dash. Her skinny figure didn't give off much of an athletic impression as she stood ready at the starting line, which was, coincidentally, right in front me.

On your mark! Dora throws her glasses down and touches the ground. *Get set.* Just then, I see her eyes. Her eyes, slanted at the corners. Her eyelashes full and long. Her pupils radiating a light brown hue. *Go!* Dora starts running. Her slender yet strong legs push against the ground with a cloud of dust, retreating farther. She is faster than anyone else. She is like the wind. A powerful yet light wind. She finishes the lap in a flash. She passes the finish line and, right before she stops, she snaps the glasses and puts them back on her nose, her mysterious eyes vanishing behind them.

Dora was usually surrounded by people and ate with a group. The groups weren't always the same. She wasn't a loner but she wasn't necessarily attached to certain friends, either. She didn't seem to care who she ate with or who she walked home with. Sometimes she was by herself. Still, she wasn't bullied and never looked out of place. She seemed like someone who could exist on her own.

53

Mom opened her eyes. After nine months in bed. The doctors said there was no need to be excited. Just because Mom had opened her eyes didn't mean she had come back. They said it was not unlike the urine tube filling up on its own. She still needed to be turned over every two hours or so with the tube attached. When she was awake, though, her eyes would rest on the ceiling, blinking. Her pupils even seemed to move, however weakly.

Mom was a person who could find constellations even from a dizzy wallpaper. *Look, doesn't the ladle shape here look like the Big Dipper? There's Cassiopeia. That's the Great Bear. Let's find the Little Bear.* Then Granny would say, *"If you're so crazy about the stars, why don't you fetch a bowl of water and pray to the moon goddess!"* I could almost hear her saucy voice. When I went to visit Granny's grave later, it was covered with weeds. I thought of Mom's and Granny's laughter, like distant echoes.

I barely had customers at the bookstore for quite some time. I still always sat behind the cash register after school but it was pointless to expect any sales. I couldn't keep living off Dr. Shim's charity forever. I realized one day that, without my mom and grandmother, the bookstore was like a grave. A grave of books. A grave of forgotten letters. That was when I decided to close down the place.

I told Dr. Shim I'd like to pack up the bookstore, downsize my belongings, and move to a room in a shared house. He was silent for a while, then instead of asking why, he just nodded.

The school librarian was a senior-class homeroom teacher who taught Korean literature. When I went to the teachers' lounge, I saw him bowing low to the vice principal, who was grilling him about his class having the lowest scores again on the last mock college exams. When he came back to his desk, his face flushed, I asked if I could donate books to the school library. He nodded absently.

The hallway was dead silent. The midterm exam season was coming up soon, and no one was making a sound during evening classes. I headed to the library, carrying the box full of books I had left in the corner of the school gymnasium earlier that morning.

The door slid open with ease. As soon as it did, spirited shouts hit my ears. *Haphaphaphap.* I walked closer to the shelves and saw a girl in profile. One foot in front, the other foot behind her, she was switching her feet back and forth as she jumped in place. Her strides were quite wide, considering that she was jumping in place. Beads of sweat gathered on her nose, her hair fluttered, and our eyes met. It was Dora.

"Hi," I said. It was polite to say hi first in these types of situations. Dora stopped. "I'm here to donate books." I opened the box, answering a question she hadn't asked.

"Just leave it there. I'm sure the librarians will organize the books for you," she said.

"Aren't you a student librarian?"

"I'm on the track team."

"Does our school have an official track team?"

"Yes, although there's no teacher in charge and I'm the only member."

"Oh." I slowly put down my half-open box in a corner.

"Where did you get all these books?"

I told her about the bookstore. Most of the books I'd brought were test-prep books. As test-prep books went in and out of fashion, outdated ones didn't sell well unless they were famous.

"By the way," I asked, "why are you practicing here and not in the gym?"

Dora had been walking with her hands clasped behind her back when she whipped around. "That place is too exposed. It's quiet here. Kids barely come here, you know. And I need a basic workout to run faster."

People's eyes light up when they talk about things they love. Dora's were radiant.

"What's the running for?" I wasn't asking with any specific intention. But her eyes were extinguished at once.

"Do you know you just asked the question I hate most? I've had it enough with my parents asking that."

"I'm sorry. I wasn't trying to judge you, I just wanted to know your purpose. Your purpose for running."

Dora let out a sigh. "To me, that's like being asked, *Why do you live?* Do you live for any purpose? Let's be honest, we just live because we're alive. When things are great we're happy, and when things aren't, we cry. Same with running. I'll be happy when I win, I'll be sad when I don't. When I feel I haven't got it, I'll blame myself or regret starting this in the first place. But then I'll still run. Just because! Like living life. That's all!"

Dora had started out calm but by the end she was almost shouting. I nodded to calm her down.

"Are your parents persuaded by that?"

"No, they just laugh at me. They say running is useless—there's no need for it when I become an adult, other than for rushing to cross the street before the traffic light changes. Funny, right? They tell me I'm no Usain Bolt, so why bother running." The corners of her mouth drooped.

"What do your parents want you to do?"

"No idea. Before, they said if I wanted to be an athlete so much, I should play golf because at least it has a chance of making money. But now, not even that. They just tell me not to embarrass them. It was their choice to have me, but that doesn't mean that I have to accomplish the missions they've set up. They keep threatening me that I'll regret this, but even if I do regret it, that's my choice to make. I think I'm just living up to my name. They named me Dora, so I guess I just have to be a *dorai*, a 'freak.'"

She smiled, as if she felt good after ranting. I was heading out of the library when she asked me where my bookstore was. I gave her the address and asked why she wanted to know.

She grinned. "Just in case they stop letting me practice here."

54

My mock exam scores were always average. Math was my strongest subject, followed by science and social studies, which were okay. The problem was Korean. There were all these hidden meanings and nuances that I couldn't catch. Why were the authors' motives kept hidden so well? My guesses were always wrong.

Maybe understanding a language is like understanding the expressions and emotions of other people. That's why they say small amygdalae often mean your intellectual level is lower. Because you can't grasp the context, your reasoning skills are poor and so is your intellect. It was hard for me to accept my Korean grades. It was the subject I wanted to be best at, but it was my worst.

Clearing out the bookstore took some time. All I needed to do was get rid of the books but it was no easy task. I took out each book and took pictures one by one. I needed to check their conditions so that I could post them on a bartering website. I had no idea we had so many books in the store. Countless thoughts, stories, and studies were piled up on every shelf. I thought of the authors I'd never had a chance to meet. Suddenly they seemed very far from me, a thought that hadn't occurred to me before. I used to think that they were close. As close as soaps or towels, easily within reach. But, in fact, no, they were in a whole other world. Maybe forever out of my reach.

"Hey."

I heard a voice over my shoulder. My heart froze at that one word, as if someone had just splashed cold water on me. It was Dora.

"Just swinging by. That's cool, right?"

"Probably. Actually, it always is," I corrected myself. "It's rare to hear a customer asking for permission to visit, unless it's at a popular restaurant that requires a reservation, I guess . . . which this is clearly not."

I realized I had just ended up calling my bookstore unpopular. Dora burst out laughing for some reason. It was the kind of laugh that sounded like countless ice crystals showering down onto the ground. Dora skimmed through the books, a smile still tugging at the corners of her mouth.

"Did this shop just open? The books are all over the place."

"Actually, I'm preparing to close it down. Though 'preparing' seems like an odd word to use when you're closing down a shop."

"Too bad. I missed my chance to become a regular."

Dora didn't talk much at first. She did other things instead, like puffing out her cheeks after saying something, then making a *pfff* sound with a long deep breath. Or tapping the ground with the toe of her sneaker three times. Then, as if she had been working up the nerve for it, she asked a question.

"Is it true that you don't feel anything?" It was the same question Gon had asked.

"Not exactly, but according to general standards, yes, probably."

"Interesting. I thought those kinds of people were only in charity documentaries for fund-raising. Oh, sorry . . . I shouldn't have said it this way."

"That's okay, I don't mind."

Dora drew in a sharp breath. "You know how you asked me why I run? I feel bad for venting to you then. I came here to apologize. It's just that you were the first person to ask me that question besides my parents."

"Oh."

"So I want to ask you something too, just out of curiosity. What do you want to be when you grow up?"

I couldn't come up with an answer for a while. If I remembered correctly, that was the first time I'd been asked that question. So I just said truthfully, "I don't know. Because no one has asked me that before."

"Do you need someone to ask you that to know? Haven't you ever thought about it?"

"It's a hard question for me." I hesitated. But instead of pushing me to elaborate, Dora found something we shared in common.

"Same here. Right now my dream has kinda *evaporated*. My parents are so against running, so . . . It's sad that we share that in common."

Dora kept bending and stretching her knees. She couldn't stay still, as if she had an itch for running. Her uniform skirt fluttered. I looked away and got back to organizing the books.

"You handle them so carefully. You really love books, don't you?"

"Yeah. I'm bidding them farewell."

Dora puffed out her cheeks with another *pfff.* "Books aren't my thing. Words are no fun. They just sit there, embedded. I prefer things that move."

Dora swiftly slid her fingers along the shelved books. *Pitter-patter.* It sounded like rain dripping.

"Old books seem all right, though. They have a richer scent that's more alive. Like how autumn leaves smell." Dora grinned at her own words. Then, with a quick "See ya," she left before I could reply.

55

I was heading back home after school. It was a long sunny afternoon. The air was cold and the sun looked down on the earth from a faraway distance. No, maybe I was wrong. Maybe the sun was scorching and the sweltering heat was unbearable. I strolled along the gray school fence and was about to turn a corner. There came a gush of wind. It was a strong blow, coming out of nowhere. Tree branches shook violently, letting their leaves quiver.

If my ears were working correctly, the sound wasn't from the wind shaking the trees. It was the sound of waves. In a second, leaves of every color were scattered on the ground. It was still high summer, on a sunny day, but for some reason there were fallen leaves everywhere in sight. Orange and yellow leaves cupped their hands toward the sky.

There in the distance stood Dora. The wind swept her hair to the left. Long and shiny hair, each strand as thick as string. She slowed down but I kept up my pace, so eventually we drew close. We had talked a few times before, but I had never seen her so up close. A few freckles sprinkled her fair complexion and her eyes were squinting to avoid the wind, revealing a small double eyelid. When her eyes met mine, they grew wide.

Suddenly, the wind changed course. Dora's hair slowly changed direction too, whipping over to the opposite side. The breeze carried her scent to my nose. It was a scent I hadn't smelled before. It smelled like fallen leaves, or the first buds in spring. The kind of smell that evoked contrary images all at once. I continued to walk forward. Our faces were an inch apart now. Her hair flapped in my face. *Ah*, I moaned. It prickled. A heavy rock dropped down in my heart. An unpleasant weight.

"I'm sorry," she said.

"It's okay," I said. The words, half stuck in my chest, came out in a croak. The wind pushed me hard. To resist it, I started walking faster than I had before.

———

That night I couldn't sleep. Scenes kept replaying in my head like hallucinations. The waving trees, the colorful leaves, and Dora standing there, yielding to the wind.

I got up and absently walked along the bookshelves. I took out a dictionary and searched it through. But I had no idea what word I was looking for. My body was burning. My pulse beat so loud right below my ears. I could hear my pulse even in the tips of my fingers and toes, which tingled as if bugs were crawling all over my body. It wasn't very pleasant. My head hurt and I felt dizzy. Yet I kept thinking back to that moment. The moment when her hair touched my face. The scent and the warmth of the air between us. I drifted off to sleep only at daybreak when the sky turned sapphire.

56

My fever came down by morning. But another bizarre symptom appeared. I went to school and saw the back of someone's head glowing. It was Dora's. I turned away. That whole day I felt as if a thorn were pricking my chest.

Gon stopped by the bookstore around sundown. I couldn't talk to him or even listen to what he was saying.

"Dude, you okay? You look pale."

"It hurts."

"What hurts?"

"I don't know. Everything."

Gon suggested we eat out but I turned him down. He smacked his lips then disappeared. My body felt heavy as I twisted and turned. I couldn't tell what was wrong with me. I headed out of the bookstore when I bumped right into Dr. Shim.

"Did you eat?" he asked, and I shook my head no.

We went to a buckwheat noodle place this time. Dr. Shim added that the noodles alone wouldn't be enough for a growing teen and ordered fried jumbo shrimp too, but I didn't touch a thing. I shared all the weird changes happening in my body with him as he slowly slurped his noodles. There wasn't much to tell, but because I was rambling so much, it took twice as long as it should have.

"I took cold medicine. I think I have a cold," I managed to finish.

Dr. Shim straightened his glasses, his eyes fixed on my shaking legs.

"Well, I think you can explain in more detail."

"More detail? What do you mean?" I asked, and he grinned.

"Well, I just thought, maybe there were some things you left out because you didn't know how to accurately express them. How about you take time to go over the details, one at a time? When did you first start having your symptoms? Was there some kind of trigger?"

I narrowed my eyes and tried to think back to how it had all started.

"It was the wind."

"The wind?" Dr. Shim narrowed his eyes to mirror my expression.

"It's hard to explain, but will you still hear me out?"

"Of course."

I took a deep breath and tried to recount the events of the day before with as much detail as possible. Once out loud, my story sounded rather dry and boring—that the wind blew and the leaves fell, and when her hair blew and touched my cheek, I felt as though someone were squeezing my heart. My story had no context; it wouldn't even qualify as small talk. But as I rambled on, I noticed Dr. Shim's face soften, and by the time I finished, he had a wide smile on his face. He held out his hand and I took it reflexively. He gave me a firm handshake.

"Congratulations! You're growing. This is great news." Beaming, he continued, "How much taller have you gotten since early this year?"

"Three and a half inches."

"See? That's a huge growth in such a short time. I'm sure your brain must have drastically changed as well. If I were a neurosurgeon, I would suggest you get an MRI scan and check the progress of your brain."

I shook my head. Getting pictures taken of my brain was not a pleasant memory.

"I don't plan on getting one yet. I want to wait until my amygdalae grow big enough. Actually, I don't even know if this is something to celebrate. It's uncomfortable. I also didn't get enough sleep."

"That's what happens when you have a crush on somebody."

"Do you think I have a crush on her?" I regretted asking him the question as soon as I asked.

"Well. Only your heart knows," he said, still smiling.

"You mean my brain, not my heart. We do whatever the brain tells us to do."

"Technically, yes, but we still say it's from our heart."

———

As Dr. Shim said, I was changing little by little. I had more questions, but I didn't feel like sharing all of them with Dr. Shim as I had before. I babbled and got tongue-tied with even simple questions. I started doodling, hoping it would clear my thoughts. But somehow I kept writing down not sentences but the same word

over and over again. When I realized what I had written, I immediately crumpled up the paper or leaped from my seat.

My annoying symptoms continued. No, they actually got worse
with each day. My temples throbbed at the sight of Dora, and my
ears pricked up when I heard her voice from however far away,
among however many people. I felt my body had outpaced my
mind, and that it was as unnecessary and bothersome as a long
overcoat in summer. I wanted so much to take it off. If only I
could.

57

Dora started coming by the bookstore often. The time of her visits was irregular. Sometimes she would turn up on a weekend and sometimes on a weeknight. But always around the time she was about to visit, my backbone would ache. Like an animal instinctively sensing an impending earthquake, like a worm squirming out of the earth before a rainstorm.

Whenever I felt my body itch, I would walk out of the bookstore, and there she would appear, the tip of her head rising into view from the horizon. I would scramble back inside as if I'd just seen something ominous, then I would go about my work as if nothing had happened.

Dora said she would help clear out the books, but when she found a book she liked, she would sit reading the same page for a long time. She was interested in encyclopedias of animals, insects, and nature. Dora found beauty in everything. She found nature's magnificent work and incredible symmetry in a turtle's carapace, or a stork's egg, or an autumn reed from a swamp. *How wonderful*, she would often say. I understood the meaning of the word, but I could never feel the splendor it carried.

As fall ripened and the books were being sorted out, Dora

and I talked about the cosmos, flowers, and nature—how big the universe is, how there's a flower that eats insects by melting them, and how some fish swim upside down.

"You know what? We assume all dinosaurs are huge, but there were some as small as a double bass, called *Compsognathus*. They must've been so cute," said Dora, a colorful children's book spread open on her knees.

"I used to read this book when I was little. My mom read it to me," I said.

"Do you remember your mom reading it to you?"

I nodded. *Hypsilophodon* were the ones as big as a bathtub, *Microceratus* were as big as a puppy, *Micropachycephalosaurus* was around nineteen inches tall, and *Mussaurus* were the size of a small teddy bear. I remembered all these long, strange names.

The corners of Dora's lips turned upward.

"Do you go see your mom often?" she asked.

"Yeah, every day."

She hesitated for a moment. "Can I come too?"

"Sure," I blurted out even before thinking.

———

A small stuffed dinosaur sat by a window in Mom's hospital ward. Dora had bought it on the way. I hadn't brought anyone here before. I knew Dr. Shim stopped by every so often, but neither of us had ever suggested visiting Mom together. Dora leaned over, smiling, and carefully held Mom's hands. She stroked them.

"Hello, Mrs. Seon. I'm Dora, Yunjae's friend. You're so beautiful. Yunjae is doing great at school, all healthy and well. You should wake up and see him. I'm sure you will soon."

Then she stepped back, her smile fading a little. She whispered to me, "Now it's your turn."

"What?"

"Do what I just did."

"Mom can't hear anything anyway," I said in a normal voice, unlike Dora, who had lowered hers.

"It's no big deal. It's just saying hi." She gave me a gentle push.

Slowly, I took a few steps toward Mom. She looked exactly the same as she had for the last couple of months. I could barely open my mouth. I hadn't tried this before.

"Do you want some time alone with her? I can leave."

"No."

"Or if I'm pushing you too much . . ."

Just then, the word "Mom" came out of my mouth. I began to share with her all that had happened to me. Come to think of it, there were a lot of things I hadn't told her. Of course there were, as this was my first time telling her anything. I slowly opened up to her. That Granny had passed away and I was left alone. That I was going to high school now. I told her that I met new friends like Gon and Dora. That winter, spring, and summer had passed and it was now fall already. That I'd tried to keep the bookstore going and that I had to close it down, but that I wouldn't apologize for that.

After telling Mom all this, I stepped back. Dora smiled at me. Mom was still staring up at the constellations on the ceiling, but I realized that talking to her wasn't so pointless after all. Maybe it was similar to how Dr. Shim baked for his dead wife.

58

As I grew closer to Dora, I started to feel like I was keeping a secret from Gon. Incidentally, the two had never stopped by the bookstore at the same time. Gon didn't come to the bookstore as often as he used to, maybe he was busy with other stuff. When he did, he always sniffed. "Something smells fishy about you."

"What do you mean?"

"I can't put my finger on it." He scowled at me. "You hiding something from me?"

"Well . . ." I would've told him about Dora if he had pushed me further. But for some reason, Gon stopped there.

It was also around that time that Gon started hanging out with kids from different schools. They were fairly well-known troublemakers in the neighborhood. Some of them had gone to the same juvenile center as Gon. A kid called Steamed Bun was particularly infamous among them. I once saw him talking to Gon after school. Unlike his nickname, he actually reminded me of bamboo. He was tall like a bamboo plant, and his arms and legs were skinny like the branches. But at the tips of those branches were hands and feet that were thick buns. He was like a stick doll whose hands and feet were made of thick batter. But the real reason he'd gotten the nickname was that with those huge fists and feet of his, he could squash the faces of people he didn't like as easily as if they were soft steamed buns.

"I like hanging out with them. There's a connection between us. You know why? Because at least they don't judge me the way other people do, telling me to do this and that."

Gon told me the stories he'd heard from Steamed Bun's gang and thought they were funny, but I didn't find them funny or interesting at all. Gon went on and on, laughing out loud, gabbling nonsense. I just listened. That was all I could do.

Gon was still being scrutinized at school. Parents continued to call in to complain about his behavior. I knew that if he got in trouble again, he might have to transfer to another school. Even though Gon was actually just sleeping through classes instead of causing trouble, his reputation still worsened. I often heard kids talking behind his back.

"Should I go ahead and stir up real shit? Feels like that's what everybody's waiting for." Gon chewed gum noisily, acting nonchalantly. I thought it was just one of his silly jokes. But he wasn't joking. By the middle of the second semester, Gon started to change. He seemed to be doing everything he could to throw himself into the abyss. He started cussing at whoever met his eyes, like he used to at the beginning of the year. In class, he sat haughtily in his chair, one leg crossed over the other, and deliberately paid no attention to teachers. When they told him off, he glared at them and pretended to correct his behavior, and they moved on without further comment to resume their class in peace.

Whenever Gon behaved like that, I felt a sudden, heavy rock sinking in my heart. Kind of like when Dora's hair had touched my skin. But this was different, heavier and ominous.

59

It was early November. A downpour brought us into late autumn. I was almost done clearing out the bookstore. I had sold all the books I could sell, and the rest were to be thrown away. I was going to leave this place soon. I had found a room in a shared apartment and was going to stay at Dr. Shim's place until I moved there. Looking at the empty bookstore, I felt like a chapter of my life had come to a close.

I turned off the light and breathed in the book smell that still lingered. It was as familiar as the background surrounding me. But I noticed something slightly different carried on the scent. Suddenly a small ember was rekindled in my heart. I wanted to read between the lines. I wanted to be someone who truly understood the meaning of an author's words. I wanted to know more people, to be able to engage in deep conversations, and to learn what it was to be human.

At that moment, Dora came into the bookstore. I didn't say hi. I wanted to tell her about my small ember before it went out.

"Do you think I could write someday? About myself?"

Dora's eyes tickled my cheeks. I continued, "Do you think I could make others understand me, even though I can't understand myself?"

"Understand," Dora whispered, turning to me. Before I knew it, she was right below my chin. Her breath touched my neck and my heart started pounding.

"Hey, your heart's beating fast," Dora murmured. Each syllable from her full lips tickled my jaw. I inhaled deeply without meaning to, drinking in her breath.

"Do you know why your heart rate is so high now?"

"No."

"Your heart's excited because I'm close to you, so it's clapping."

"Oh."

Our eyes met. But neither of us averted each other's gaze. She moved closer to me, her eyes locked on mine. Before I had time to think, her lips brushed against my lips. They felt like a cushion. Her soft, moist lips slowly pressed into mine. And just like that, we breathed three times. Our chests moved up and down, and up and down, and up and down. Then we lowered our heads at the same time. Our lips parted as our foreheads touched.

"I think I just understood a little about who you are," Dora said, gazing down at the floor. I was also looking down. Her shoelaces were untied. One end was hiding under my shoe.

"You're nice. And you're normal. But you're also special. That's how I understand you."

Dora looked up, her cheeks flushed. "Am I," she whispered, "qualified to be in your story now?"

"Maybe."

She laughed. "That's not a good enough answer." Then she skipped out the door.

My knees gave up and I slowly slumped down. My head had

emptied of thoughts, filled only with racing pulses. My whole body was beating like a drum. *Stop it. Stop. You don't have to try so hard to prove that I'm alive.* I wanted to tell my body if only I could. I shook my head a couple times. There were more and more things I couldn't expect in life. Just then, I felt someone staring and looked up. Gon was standing outside the window. We stared at each other for a few seconds. A faint smile ran across his face. Then he turned around and slowly disappeared from view.

60

Our school field trip was to Jeju Island. Some kids didn't want to go, but just because you didn't want to go did not qualify as a valid excuse. Only three students from the entire school didn't go, including myself. The other two were competing in math contests, and as for me, I had to look after Mom, which was an excuse the school had to accept.

I went to the empty school and read books all day long. As a formality, a substitute science teacher was there to take attendance. Three days passed, and the kids came back. For some reason, everyone seemed uneasy.

Something had happened on the last day of the trip. The night before the kids were due back, while everyone was asleep, the money that had been collected to buy class snacks had disappeared. The teachers searched through everyone's belongings and found the cash envelope inside Gon's backpack. It had half the original amount. Gon pleaded innocence. He actually had an alibi. He had snuck out to the Jeju streets and stayed out until the following morning. A local *PC bang* owner was his witness. Gon had spent all night at the Internet cafe, playing games and drinking beer.

Still, everyone said that Gon had stolen the money. Whether

he had made someone else steal it or plotted the theft as part of a group didn't matter. It was Gon who did it. Everyone said so.

Gon didn't care. He continued to sleep through his classes after returning from the trip. That afternoon, Professor Yun was summoned to the school. Kids said he had reimbursed all the money. They had their noses buried in their phones all day, texting one another. Their Kakao Talk buzzed here and there. I didn't have to read their texts to know what they were gossiping about.

61

Things came to a head several days later, during Korean class. Gon had woken up mid-nap and walked drowsily to the back of the classroom. The teacher ignored him and carried on with the class. Then the class heard a loud noise of chewing gum. Of course, it was Gon.

"Spit it out," said the teacher, who was retiring soon and did not tolerate bad behavior. Gon didn't respond. The sound of his chewing pierced the heavy, silent air.

"Spit it out or leave." As soon as the teacher said it, Gon spat out the gum. It drew a parabola and landed on someone's shoe. The teacher slammed his textbook shut.

"Follow me."

"What if I don't want to?" Gon said, leaning his back against the wall, clasping his hands behind his head. "What can you do anyway? Take me to the teachers' lounge and threaten me? Or call that douchebag who calls himself my dad? If you wanna hit me, go ahead. If you wanna swear at me, go ahead. What's stopping you, huh? Be honest with yourselves for once! You fucktards."

The teacher didn't bat an eyelid, something he had possibly learned through decades of teaching. He just stared at Gon for a couple of seconds and then walked out of the classroom. Chaos erupted in his wake. Silent chaos, in which each of us just stared down at our books.

"Any of you assholes wanna earn some money? Come on out," Gon said with a sly snicker. "Anyone wanna take some beating for cash? I'll pay you depending on how hard I beat you. A punch in the face is a hundred thousand *won*. If you bleed, you get an extra five hundred. Two million for a broken bone. Any takers?"

The classroom was filled with the sound of Gon's heavy breathing.

"Why so quiet, huh? Aren't you little shits up for extra cash to buy snacks? How are you gonna survive in this tough world when you're all a bunch of pussies? Stupid, useless motherfuckers!"

He emphasized that last word so hard that it echoed out into the hallway. His body was trembling and a disturbing smile played across his lips as they twitched. Frankly, he looked like he was about to cry.

"Stop," I said. Gon's eyes sparked.

"What did you say?" He stood up straight with his fists clenched. "Stop, then what? Should I like, bow and apologize, or write an apology letter or something? Should I fuckin' crawl on four legs and beg for forgiveness? Why don't you tell me exactly what to do? What should I do, fucking asshole!"

I couldn't say anything. Because Gon was hurling everything he could get his hands on. The shrilling *eek*s of the girls and the low, panicked *uhh*s of the boys created a strange dissonant chorus that pierced my ears. Gon trashed the classroom in a matter of seconds. Desks and chairs were thrown upside down and the frames and timetables mounted on the wall hung crooked. It was like Gon had grabbed the whole classroom and shaken it up. The kids stuck close to the wall as if there had been an earthquake. Just then, I heard a sound. Soft but clear, yet it was as earsplitting as a scream.

"You piece of trash . . ."

Gon turned toward the sound. Dora stood there.

"Get lost. Don't stir shit up here. Go back to where you belong."

Her face wore an expression I couldn't quite comprehend. Her eyes, her nose, her lips were all doing something different. Her eyebrows had shot up, and her nostrils were slightly flared. Her lips were curled but for some reason they were trembling.

Just then, the classroom door flung open as the homeroom teacher came rushing in, accompanied by several other teachers. But before they could do anything, Gon had already slipped out the back door. Nobody called him back or went after him. Not even me.

62

Gon showed up at the bookstore that night. He carelessly banged on the empty bookshelves as he talked to me.

"What a player. The robot has a girlfriend now, huh? How does it feel to have a girl who sticks up for you? I was literally struck dumb when she told me to get lost. Lucky bastard, I'm jealous you're getting so much of what you can't even feel."

I was speechless. With a dismissive wave of his hand, Gon said, "Hey, no need to get all tensed up, it's just you and me." Then looking straight into my eyes, he said, "But I have a question." Finally getting to the point: "Do you also think I did it?"

"You know I didn't even go on the field trip."

"Just answer me. Do you think it was me who stole the money?"

"Are you asking me about the possibility?"

"Yeah, if you say so. The possibility that I did it."

"Well, it's possible that anyone who was there could've done it."

"And I'm by far the most likely one?" He nodded with a smile.

"If you're asking for my honest opinion," I said slowly, "I'm not surprised that everyone thought it was you. They have plenty of reasons to think so. They probably can't think of anyone else."

"I see. I thought so too. That's why I didn't bother insisting I was innocent. You know, I told them, just once, that it wasn't me. But it was useless. I didn't want to waste my breath so I kept my mouth shut. But then that 'father' of mine just went right ahead and paid off the stolen money without even asking me. Must've been at least a couple hundred thousand *won*. Should I be proud of having such a father?"

I didn't say a word. Gon remained silent for a while too.

"But you know I didn't do it," he said, his tone inflecting slightly upward at the end of his sentence. A beat of silence went by. "So anyway, maybe I should live exactly as people expect me to live. That's what I'm great at, anyway."

"What are you talking about?"

"I told you last time, I want to be strong. I've thought a lot about this. About what I should do to get strong. I could either study hard or work out and make myself strong. But you know, that's not my thing. It's too late. I'm too old."

"You're too old?" I repeated after him. *Old*. As I looked at him, for a moment I really thought he might be right.

"Yeah, I'm too old. Too old to go back."

"So?" I asked.

"So, I'm going to be stronger. In my own way. In the way that feels most natural to me. I like to win. If I can't protect myself from being hurt, I'd rather hurt other people."

"How?"

"Dunno, but it won't be too hard. I'm already familiar with that kind of world." Gon sniggered. I wanted to say something but he was already heading out the door. Then he wheeled around and said, "We might not see each other from now on. So instead of a goodbye kiss, take this." He winked and slowly raised his middle finger. He wore a soft smile. That was the last time I saw him smile that way. Then he disappeared.

And then, tragedy unfolded rapidly.

PART FOUR

63

The real thief turned out to be someone else. It was the boy at the beginning of the school year who had asked out loud how I'd felt seeing Granny killed before my eyes. He went to the homeroom teacher and admitted that he'd planned everything by himself. His purpose was not the money, but to set someone up just to see how people would react. When the homeroom teacher asked him why he would do such a thing, he simply replied, "Thought it might be fun."

But that didn't mean the kids felt sorry for Gon. *Whatever, Yun Leesu would've stirred up trouble sooner or later.* I glimpsed such messages over my shoulder in the chats on their phones.

Professor Yun looked gaunt, as if he hadn't eaten for days. He leaned against the wall and moved his dry, cracked lips.

"I've never hit anyone in my whole life. I've never thought a beating would solve anything. But, but I beat Leesu. Twice. I couldn't think of any other way to stop him."

"One time was at the pizzeria. I saw you through the window," I said.

He nodded. "I made a settlement with the restaurant owner.

Fortunately, no one was injured, and the matter was resolved. That night, I forced him to get in the car and we went home. We didn't speak a word on our way back or after we got home. I just went straight to my room." His voice began to tremble. "Things have changed a lot since Leesu returned. I didn't even have the time to grieve over my wife's death. She might have dreamed of a home where all of us lived together. But actually I found it difficult to be living with Leesu. I couldn't stop thinking even as I read books or lay on my bed: *What made him grow up like that? Who on earth should be blamed?*"

Professor Yun took a few deep breaths before adding, "When sadness and disappointment get out of control, and there is no solution, people start thinking bad thoughts. I did too . . . I often imagined what it would've been like if he wasn't here, if he'd never come back . . ."

His shoulders began to heave.

"You know what the worst part is? I've actually thought that things might've been better than they are now if we'd never had him, if that boy had never been born. Yes, I've had such terrible thoughts about my son, my own flesh and blood. Oh my, I can't believe I just told you all this . . ."

Tears streaked down his neck and rolled onto his sweater. Soon he was sobbing so hard I couldn't make out what he was saying. I made a cup of hot chocolate and handed it to him.

"I heard you were close friends with Leesu. That you came over to our house once. How could you still treat him like that? After everything he did to you."

"Because Gon is a good kid."

"You think so?"

Yes. I know. That Gon is a good kid. But if someone asked me to talk about him in more detail, I'd only be able to say that he beat me and hurt me, he ripped apart a butterfly, he set his face against the teachers, and threw things at my classmates. That's how language is. It is as hard as proving that Leesu and Gon are the same person. So, I simply said, "I just know he is."

Professor Yun smiled at my words. The smile lasted for about three seconds and suddenly broke. Because he started crying again.

"Thank you, for thinking of him that way."

"Then why are you crying?"

"Because I feel sorry I couldn't think of him the same way. And because it's ridiculous that I feel grateful hearing someone else say he's a good person . . ." he stammered, sobbing. Just before he left, he asked one last thing, a little hesitantly.

"If you ever hear from him, could you give him my words? To please come back?"

"Why do you want me to say those words?"

"Well, I'm embarrassed to say this as an adult. But things happened one after another without stopping. And I had no time to devote attention to and care for each one. I would like another chance to get things right this time," he said.

"I'll tell him," I promised.

———

All kinds of thoughts went through my mind. If Professor Yun could go back in time, would he have chosen not to have Gon? If he had, the couple wouldn't have lost Gon in the first place. Mrs. Yun wouldn't have been ill from guilt and died of regret. All the trouble Gon caused wouldn't have happened either. If you think about it that way, then it would've been better if Gon had never been born. Because, more than anything, he wouldn't have had to feel so much pain and loss. But everything loses its meaning if you think that way. Only purpose remains. Barren.

———————

It was early dawn, but I was still wide awake. I had something to tell Gon. I had to say I was sorry. Sorry for pretending to be his mother's son, sorry for keeping from him that I'd made another friend. And finally, sorry for not telling him that I knew he didn't steal the money and that I believed him.

64

I had to find Gon. That meant first I'd have to find that kid called Steamed Bun.

The school he went to was in the middle of a red-light district. It was surprising that anyone would ever decide to build a school there, of all places. Maybe the seediness of the district developed after the school was built, but still. The yellow-brown rays of the afternoon sun stretched across the schoolyard, where kids who looked nothing like students were smoking.

A few kids prowling around the school entrance shoved me on my way in. I told them I'd come to see Steamed Bun. He was the only one I could ask about where Gon might be. He might know the kinds of places that would welcome Gon.

Steamed Bun walked toward me from a distance. He was skinny and his shadow looked like a skewer. Up close, his hands and feet and face were so huge they looked like fruit dangling from branches. At his nod, the other kids began taking turns prodding my ribs and searching my pockets. Once Steamed Bun realized I had nothing to offer, he asked, "What does a Goody Two-shoes like you want with me?"

"Gon isn't around. I thought you might know where he is. Don't worry, whatever you say, I won't tell the grown-ups."

Unexpectedly, he answered right away: "Steel Wire." He shrugged, cocking his head left and right a couple times with a loud *crack*. "That bastard must've gone to Steel Wire. I'm telling ya, I have nothing to do with this. Steel Wire is out of my league. I'm still a student, after all," said Steamed Bun as he turned and tapped his backpack.

"Where is he?" I simply asked, as the name Steel Wire didn't roll off the tongue yet.

Steamed Bun's cheek twitched. "Why? You gonna go after him? I don't recommend it."

"Yes," I replied curtly. I had no time to fool around. *Tsk Tsk*, Steamed Bun clicked, and hesitated for a while before he finally gave me the name of a port town not too far from our city.

"There's a farmer's market there, and at the end of it you'll see an old shoe store. All I know is they sell dance shoes. I haven't been there myself. Good luck. Although it'll be useless." Steamed Bun made a gun with his fingers, pointed it at my head, and mouthed *bang*, before he swaggered out of sight.

65

Dora stopped by before I went to find Gon. She sat there for a long while before she apologized.

"I didn't know you were close to Leesu. If I had known, I wouldn't have said that to him. Still, someone needed to speak up and stop him." She started out soft but by the end her voice was strong. "I still can't wrap my head around it. How did you end up becoming friends with someone like him . . ." she mumbled.

Someone like him. Yes, that was what everybody must've thought of Gon. I was one of them. I told Dora the same thing I had said to Dr. Shim. That if I understood Gon, I thought I could somehow understand what happened to Mom and Granny. I wanted to give it a try so that I could unlock at least one secret in life.

"So did you find out?"

I shook my head. "But I found something else."

"What?"

"Gon."

Dora shrugged and shook her head.

"But why do *you* have to go searching for him?" she asked for the last time.

"Because I've realized he is my friend."

That was my answer.

66

The sea breeze was salty and fishy. The kind of smell that erased the seasons and directions altogether. I sneaked into the farmer's market as if I was being pushed by the wind. People were in line for a popular sweet-and-sour chicken place.

It turned out Steamed Bun wasn't great at giving directions. I asked around for the dance shoes store, but it was nowhere to be found. I wandered in the market for a long time before I stumbled into an alley that seemed more like a maze. It was a dizzying tangle and I went wherever my feet took me.

Darkness in winter settled quickly. One moment you noticed it gathering, the next moment everything turned inky black. I heard a strange sound from somewhere. It sounded like a squeak, or a newborn puppy's cry. Then the sound was layered with a few more voices and laughter. I turned to the sound and saw a half-open entrance to a dark building. It was a shoddy iron gate, swaying in the wind. I heard snickers. Suddenly, a strange chill crept down my spine. I tried to think of a word that would describe the feeling. This was familiar. But I couldn't think of the word.

Just then, the gate creaked open and a group of kids came rushing out. I quickly hid behind the wall. They looked around my age or a few years older, giggling as they vanished into the night. Again, a familiar feeling crept over me.

There, I caught sight of a high heel lying in front of the door. A fancy shoe covered in gold sparkles. I flipped it over and saw soft leather glued to its sole. It looked like a Latin dance shoe. As if the shoe was showing me where to go, there was a set of stairs leading below. I padded down the stairs in the dark. At the foot of them were piles of boxes and another thick iron gate with a long steel latch. I stood in front of the door. I could open it from my side but the rustiness took me some time. Finally, I managed to remove the latch and opened the door.

There was clutter everywhere. Heaps of junk were littered in the dirty, shabby room. It looked like a secret hideout but I couldn't guess what was going on inside.

I heard a rustle. Then our eyes met. Gon. He sat hugging his knees on the floor. Small, pitiful Gon, more ragged than he had been, and alone. *Déjà vu.* That was the term I had been searching for. *Family Game* coursed through my mind. The shopkeeper's cry. The younger me, lost. The moment when Mom pulled me into a tight embrace at the police station. Fast-forward, and two women collapsing in front of me . . . I shook my head. Now was not the time to think of those things. Because before me was not the shopkeeper's dead son, but Gon, who was still alive.

67

Gon glared at me. Of course, I must've been the last person he expected to see there.

"What are you doing here? How did you get here, dammit . . ." he barely spat out in a gruff voice. Somehow he had bruises and scratches all over him, his face pale.

"I went to see Steamed Bun. Don't worry, I didn't tell anybody, including your dad."

Before I even finished the word "dad," Gon seized an empty can next to him and chucked it. The can flew through the air, hit the dusty ground, and spun a few times.

"What happened to *you*? Let's call the police first," I said.

"The police? You're fucking funny. Hunting me down like the fucking fuzz." Saying that, Gon burst into strange laughter. Unnecessarily loud laughter with one hand on his belly, throwing back his head and howling. He spat words like "You think I'll thank you for this?" I cut his laughter short.

"Don't laugh like that. It doesn't suit you. It doesn't even sound like laughing."

"And now you're telling me how to fucking laugh? I'll do what I wanna do and be where I wanna be so why don't you mind your own business, you fucking psycho. Who do you think you are, huh? Who the fuck do you . . ."

Gon's voice was quieting down. I waited, watching him trembling slightly. His face had changed a lot in just a few days. A black shadow had settled on his now-rough skin. Something had drastically altered him.

"Let's go home," I said.

"Fuck that. Don't act all cool. Get the fuck out of here while you can. Before it's too late," Gon growled.

"What are you going to do here? Do you think enduring all this will make you strong? This isn't strong. It's just pretending to be."

"Don't talk like you know everything, asshole. Who are you to be fucking preaching at me?" Gon shouted. But strangely, his eyes started to freeze. I heard faint footsteps. They were getting closer by the second and stopped at the gate.

"I told you to fuck off," Gon said, his face contorting. Then *he* came in.

68

He looked more like a giant shadow than a person. He could've been in his twenties or even his mid-thirties, depending on the angle. He wore a thick, shabby coat, khaki corduroy pants, and a bucket hat. His face was barely visible, as he had on a mask. It was a strange outfit. He was Steel Wire.

"Who's this?" Steel Wire asked Gon. If a snake could speak, it would've sounded like him. Gon bit his lips, so I answered for him.

"I'm his friend."

Steel Wire raised his eyebrows. A couple of wrinkles appeared on his forehead.

"How did your friend find this place? Forget that, why is your friend here?"

"To get Gon."

Slowly, Steel Wire sat down on a creaking chair. His long shadow folded in half too.

"I think you've got the wrong idea, kid. You think you're some kind of a hero?" he muttered in a low voice. His tone was soft, it could even come across as friendly, if you didn't pay attention to what he was actually saying.

"Gon's father is waiting for him. He has to go home."

"Shut up!" Gon shouted. He then whispered something to Steel Wire, who listened and nodded a few times.

"Oh, you're that kid. Gon's told me about you. I don't know if that kind of disease really exists, but no wonder your expression didn't change a bit when I walked in. Most people who see me don't react like you did."

"I'm taking Gon home," I repeated. "Let him go."

"What you gon' do, Gon? You wanna leave with your friend?"

Gon bit his lips then smirked. "You think I'm crazy? There's no way I'm leaving with that asshole."

"Great. Friendship only lasts so long. It's just a word. There are many meaningless words out there." Steel Wire stood up from the chair, bent down, and fished something out of his coat pocket. It was a sharp, slim knife. Every time its blade reflected the light, it glinted with a blinding flash.

"Remember I showed you this? Told you we could use it one day."

Gon's mouth opened slowly. Steel Wire pointed the tip of the blade at Gon.

"Have a go at it."

Gon swallowed hard. His breathing must've quickened, because his chest began to heave.

"Oh, look at you, all scared. This is just your first time, so you don't have to go all the way. Take it easy and just have fun with it."

Steel Wire grinned as he took off his hat. There, I saw a familiar face. It took me a second to realize whose face it was—either

Michelangelo's *David* or one of the many faces known for their iconic beauty I'd seen in textbooks. That same beauty was in Steel Wire's face. His skin was fair and his lips rosy. Light brown hair, and long, lush eyelashes. Deep, clear eyes. God had given the face of an angel to the wrong person.

69

Steel Wire and Gon were from the same youth detention center. They had briefly seen each other around from a distance. Steel Wire's exploits and sagas were so extreme and dangerous that they were discussed only in private. According to one rumor, Steel Wire had gotten his nickname because he used a steel wire for one of his crimes. I remember Gon telling me about Steel Wire at great length as if he were reciting the biography of some great man.

Steel Wire thought it was boring to work for other people and blend in with society. In fact, he had mapped out his own road. A road that reached a point where no one had gone before. I didn't quite understand it, but apparently many kids were captivated by that strange world, and Gon was one of them.

"Steel Wire thinks this country should legalize guns like in the U.S. and Norway, so we can have shooting sprees sometimes. That way we can wipe out the shitty people all at once. Isn't that cool? That guy is crazy strong."

"Do you think that makes him strong?"

"Of course. He's not afraid of anyone. Like you. I wanna be like that."

Gon had said this one summer night. The day when he told me everything about himself.

70

Now Gon was holding a knife in front of me. His breathing was loud, as if he were breathing into my ears. What would he do? What did he want to prove from all this? His wavering pupils glistened like large marbles.

"Let me just ask you this. Is this what you really want?" I asked quietly. But one of Gon's things is cutting someone short. He kicked me hard in the side before I could finish my words. I was slammed into the window from the force of the kick. Glass cups next to me shattered on the floor.

There are kids who boast of how young they were when they started stealing and fooling around with girls, and what landed them in the juvenile center. They need such stories or tokens to be accepted into their gangs. Gon enduring the beatings from the other kids was perhaps a rite of passage in that sense. But to me, all those things were only proof of their weakness. It was a manifestation of their vulnerability *because* they longed for strength.

The Gon I knew was just an immature fifteen-year-old boy. A weak softie who just pretended to be strong.

"I said, is this what you really want?" I asked again. Gon was panting. "Because I don't think it is."

"Shut up."

"I don't think this is what you want, Gon."

"I said, shut the fuck up."

"You are not that kind of person."

"Fuck," he shouted, half crying. A nail on the wall must've pricked my leg, because it was bleeding. Gon saw and started weeping like a child. Yes, this was who he was. The kind of person who tears up at a drop of blood, who feels pain for others' pain.

"I told you, you're not that kind."

Gon turned his back on me as he put up his elbows to cover his eyes, his body trembling.

"That's you. That's all you are," I said.

"Good for you . . . Fucking good for you that you feel nothing. I wish I could be the same . . ." he mumbled through his cries.

"Let's go." I offered my hand. "Let's get out of here."

"You go, asshole. I don't fucking know you."

Gon had finally stopped crying and started cussing at me. As if this were his only way out. He cussed like a barking dog.

"Stop." Steel Wire raised his hand to stop Gon. "No more childish drama in front of me, kids." He turned to me. "Take him if you want. But you have to give me something in return. You guys have such a wonderful friendship, surely it must be worth something to you, right?" Steel Wire quietly rubbed his chin. I could see Gon's face going pale. "So, what can you do, kid? For Gon?"

His voice was soft, his intonation rising pleasantly at the end of his sentence as he gave me a smile. I had been taught that was a gesture of kindness. But I knew he was by no means acting out of kindness.

"Anything," I said.

Steel Wire's eyes widened. He let out a low whistle as if he were surprised by my response.

"Anything?"

"Yes."

"Even if you could die?"

"Fuck," Gon said quietly. Steel Wire straightened, clearly amused.

"Okay, let's see what you've got. I'm very curious how much you're willing to take for this asshole." Steel Wire smiled. "Don't be hard on yourself if you can't take it. It just proves you're human."

Gon shut his eyes tight as Steel Wire walked closer to me. I didn't close my eyes. I looked straight at what would become of my reality.

71

People later asked me why I hadn't run away. Why I'd stayed until the end. I told them I'd only done what was easiest for me, the only thing someone who can't feel fear could do.

Like a fluorescent light flickering on and off, I slipped in and out of consciousness. When I came to, the intensity of pain was so strong. Strong enough to wonder why the human body was designed to endure so much of it. Painful enough to think it was unfair that I still hadn't fully shut down.

I saw glimpses of Gon. Sometimes in a blur, sometimes clearly. My brain must've been in error. I saw how scared he was. Now I understood a little what it meant to be frightened. It was like desperately gasping for air in a place without oxygen. That was how Gon was looking at me.

Gon's face turned blurry. I thought my sight had become fuzzy, but it hadn't. Gon's face was smudged with tears. He was wailing. *Stop, please stop. Hurt me instead.* His shout seemed endless. I wanted to shake my head to tell him that he didn't have to say that, but I was already worn out.

72

The memory flashed into my mind. The day when Gon had torn off the butterfly's wings, when he'd tried to teach me empathy but couldn't. Around dusk that day, Gon cleaned the remains of the butterfly smeared on the ground, crying all the while.

"I wish I could never feel fear, pain, guilt, everything . . ." he had said in a teary voice.

"That's not something anyone can just do. Besides, you are too full of emotions. I think you'd rather make a good artist or a musician," I'd said after some thought.

Gon had laughed, his eyes wet.

That day had been in the summer, unlike now when every gasp of pain came out as white vapor. The peak of summer. *Summer.* Had that day really existed? When everything was green and lush and full? Everything we'd experienced together, was it truly real?

———

Gon had often asked me—what it was like to be fearless. What it was like to feel nothing. Even though I struggled to explain every time, he always came back and asked me the same question.

I also had so many questions left unanswered. At first, I

wondered what went through that man's mind when he stabbed Granny. But that question led to another one. Why did people know yet pretend not to know? I had no idea what to make of them.

There was this day when I was visiting Dr. Shim. On the TV screen, a boy who had lost both his legs and an ear from a bombing was crying. A news report on a war happening somewhere in the world. Dr. Shim was watching the screen with no expression on his face. Hearing my footsteps, he turned around, greeting me with a friendly smile. My eyes were locked on the boy behind his smile. Even a fool like me can see the boy's hurt. That he's in extreme pain from a terrible, tragic incident.

But I didn't ask him. *Why are you smiling? How could you smile with your back turned on somebody in such pain?* I didn't ask.

Because I'd seen everybody else do it. Even Mom and Granny, when they flipped through the channels. Mom would say, *A tragedy that's too distant cannot be "your" tragedy.*

Fine, let's say that's true. But what about the people who did nothing as they just stood and watched Mom and Granny being attacked that day? They saw it happen in front of their eyes. They were too close to use the excuse that it was "a distant tragedy." I remembered one of the witnesses, a choir member, giving an interview. He said that the man was thrashing around in a craze, so the witness was too scared to get any closer.

People shut their eyes to a distant tragedy saying there's nothing they could do, yet they didn't stand up for one happening nearby either because they're too terrified. Most people could feel but didn't act. They said they sympathized, but easily forgot. The way I see it, that was not real.

I didn't want to live like that.

———

A strange sound slipped out of Gon's body. A deep, intense howl that rose from the pit of his stomach. It sounded like an old, rusty cogwheel creaking into motion, or the wail of a wild animal. *Why was he trying so hard to do what he was never good at?* The word "pitiful" kept tugging at the tip of my tongue.

"Is this all you've got? All right. Then don't you regret it," said Steel Wire, his eyes locked on Gon.

Steel Wire snatched something lying next to Gon. It was the knife he had handed to Gon earlier. Before either of us could do anything, Steel Wire brought it to Gon's throat. But he didn't get a chance to hurt Gon. Because it was me who took the blow of the knife. Because that was the end of it all.

73

The moment I pushed Gon aside, Steel Wire's knife dug deep into my chest. Gon kept screaming the word "demon" at Steel Wire. Steel Wire pulled out the knife. Red liquid, the warm, sticky essence oozed swiftly out of my body. I passed out shortly.

Somebody shook my shoulders. Gon was hugging me in his arms.

"Don't die. I beg you. I'll do anything for you . . . anything . . ." Gon whimpered. He was covered in blood. I glimpsed Steel Wire lying facedown on the floor. I don't know why those words came out of me. But it was then I just whispered, "Say sorry. To everyone you've hurt. To the butterfly you killed. To the bugs you've stepped on carelessly. Say you're sorry."

I had come here to apologize to Gon, and now I was telling *him* to apologize. But Gon nodded.

"I will, I will, I really will. So please . . ."

Gon held me tight as he rocked me back and forth. Then I couldn't hear his voice anymore. My eyes slowly closed. My body felt lethargic, as if I were letting myself sink into deep water. I was returning to a primordial place where I had lived before I was born. A blurry scene started to come into focus as if someone were playing a movie in my head.

A snowy day. My birthday. Mom is sprawled out on the floor, her blood soaking the snow. I see Granny. Her face is as fierce as a wild beast's. She screams from outside the window, *Go, go, get out of the way!* I'd learned the phrase usually meant *I hate you.* Like when Dora shouted at Gon, "Get lost." So why? Why was Granny telling me to go?

Blood splatters. It's Granny's blood. Everything turns red before my eyes. Had Granny been in pain? As I was now? Had she, nevertheless, been relieved that she was the one in pain, and not me?

Plop. A teardrop fell on my face. It was hot. So hot that it burned. Just then, something inside my heart exploded. Strange feelings flooded in. No, they didn't flood in, they flooded out. A dam that had existed somewhere inside my body burst. A sudden surge. Something inside me broke free, forever.

"I feel it," I whispered. Whether it was grief, happiness, loneliness, pain, fear, or joy, I did not know. I just knew I felt something. A wave of nausea hit me. I wanted to throw up the disgust that was surging into me. Yet, I thought it was a wonderful experience. Suddenly, an unbearable drowsiness overcame me. My eyes were heavy. The face of Gon, all wet with tears, vanished from sight.

At last, I became a human. And at that very moment, the world was drifting far away from me.

In fact, this is the end of my story.

74

So, what follows is a sort of postscript to my story.

My soul slipped out of my body and looked down at Gon, holding me in his arms, crying. The hairless patch on his head was shaped like a star. I realized, I had not once laughed at it. *Hahaha.* I laughed out loud. That's the last thing I remember.

When I came to, I was back in reality. Meaning, I was at the hospital. I dozed on and off for hours. It took several months for me to fully recover and start walking again.

In my sleep, I had the same recurring dream. In it, it's sports day in the schoolyard. Gon and I stand in the sun among clouds of dust. It is blazing hot. A track-and-field event is taking place in front of us. Gon grins and slides something into my hand. I spread out my fingers to find a translucent marble rolling in my palm. A red curved line through the middle looks like a smile. As I roll the marble around in my hand, the red line keeps flipping, making a sad face and a smiley face by turns. It's plum-flavored candy.

I put it in my mouth. It is sweet and sour. My mouth waters. I roll the candy around with my tongue. Sometimes it knocks against my teeth, making *click click* sounds. All of a sudden, my tongue prickles. Salty and sharp, pungent or bitter. Amid it all wafts up the sweetest scent that keeps me sniffing hungrily.

Bang! The sound of the starting pistol shakes the air. We push off the ground and break into a run. It is not a race, it's just running. All we need to do is simply feel our bodies splitting the air.

I woke up to find Dr. Shim next to me. He told me what had happened.

That day, right after I passed out, Professor Yun rushed to the scene with the police. It would've been a lot cooler if we had solved everything by ourselves, but to grown-ups, I guess we were still just kids. Dora had called our homeroom teacher and some kids had explained Gon's relationship with Steamed Bun to the police, who then sought out Steamed Bun. It was not too difficult to track Steel Wire from there.

Steel Wire was stabbed by Gon. But he was not severely injured and recovered faster than I did and was awaiting trial.

The things Steel Wire had done were beyond imaginable and it's hard to list everything here. I heard later that he smiled throughout his trial, even when he was receiving a very heavy sentence. How on earth was his mind—no, the human mind—constructed? I hoped that someday in his life he'd be given a chance to be able to wear a different expression on his face.

Dr. Shim said Gon's stabbing of Steel Wire would be considered self-defense, and that Gon was receiving therapy but wasn't ready to see me yet. Professor Yun took a leave of absence from his college to change his life and live solely for Gon. Gon still didn't talk to him much. But Professor Yun said he would never give up trying.

Dr. Shim said Dora had stopped by several times, and gave me a card she had left. I opened it to find a photo instead of any writing; that was like her, she hated letters. Dora was running in the picture. Both her legs up in midair, she looked like she was flying. She had transferred to a school that had a track-and-field team, and as soon as she did, she'd won second place in her district. I supposed she had found her dream again, the one she'd said had *evaporated*. *Dorai*, her parents must've still called her, but with a smile.

"You have more colorful expressions now," Dr. Shim told me. I shared with him the wonderful thing that had happened on that terrible night. The strange changes that my body and mind had suddenly undergone.

"Let's take an MRI when you're fully recovered," Dr. Shim said. "And redo all your clinical tests too. It's time to check how much your brain has changed. To be honest, I have always doubted your diagnosis. I was a doctor myself once, but doctors like to put labels on patients. It helps them treat abnormal symptoms, or even abnormal people. Of course, labels can often be clear and useful. But the human brain is rather a strange thing. And I still truly believe that the heart can prevail over the brain. What I'm trying to say is that you might have just grown in a way that's a little different from how other people grow." He smiled.

"Does growing mean changing?"

"Probably. For better or for worse," he replied.

I briefly recalled my last few months with Gon and Dora. And I hoped Gon would change for the better. Although I should first think about what "for the better" exactly means.

Dr. Shim said he had to go somewhere. Just before leaving the hospital ward, he first hesitated but said with a significant smile, "I don't usually like people who ruin surprises when they give out presents. But sometimes, like now, I am itching to tell you. I'll just give you a hint. You'll meet somebody in a bit. I hope you like the surprise."

He then handed me a letter from Gon.

"I'll read it after you go," I said.

I opened the envelope when Dr. Shim left. A white piece of paper was folded into a square. I slowly unfolded the letter. There were a few crude letters, written with care.

> *Sorry.*
> *Thanks.*
> *Truly.*

I stared at the period after "Truly" for a long time. I hoped that period could transform Gon's life. Would we ever meet again? I hoped so. Truly.

75

The door slid open. It was Dr. Shim again. He was pushing a wheelchair. The person sitting in it beamed at me. A familiar smile. Of course it was, I'd known it ever since I was born.

"Mom."

As soon as I said the word, Mom burst into tears. She stroked my cheeks and touched my hair, crying all the while. I didn't cry. I wasn't sure if it was because my emotional range wasn't *that* wide yet, or because my head had grown too big for that crying-in-front-of-Mom thing.

I wiped her tears and hugged her. But strangely enough, she cried even harder. While I'd been asleep, Mom had woken up, like a miracle. She had done what everyone thought was impossible. But she put it differently. That it was *me* who had done what everyone thought was impossible. I shook my head. I wanted to say more and tell her everything that had happened, but where would I begin? Suddenly, my cheeks felt warm. Mom wiped something off my cheeks. Tears. Tears were streaming down my face. I cry. And laugh, at the same time. So does Mom.

EPILOGUE

It is my eighteenth spring. I've graduated from high school and become what you call an adult.

A relaxing song is playing on the bus. People are dozing off. Spring passes by the bus window. Flowers are in bloom, whispering, *Spring, spring, I am spring.* I pass by those flowers to see Gon. Not for any particular reason or because I have something to say to him. Just because. Just to see a friend. A good friend of mine whom everyone called a monster.

From now on this is an entirely different story. Completely new and unpredictable.

———

I do not know how this story will unfold. As I said, neither you nor I nor anyone can ever know whether a story is happy or tragic. It may be impossible to categorize a story so neatly in the first place. Life takes on various flavors as it flows.

I've decided to confront it. Confront whatever life throws at me, as I always have. And however much I can feel, nothing more, nothing less.

AUTHOR'S NOTE

Four years ago in the spring, I gave birth to my baby. There are a few funny anecdotes about it, but they are not particularly emotional because I did not have a hard time giving birth. Everything just felt strange and new. But after a few days, whenever I caught sight of the baby wriggling in its cradle, I would automatically tear up. Even now, I still cannot explain why. My tears could not be explained by any single emotion.

It was just that the baby was so small. If it were to fall off from its low cradle or be left alone even for a few hours, it would not make it. This creature, who could do nothing on its own, had been thrown into this world, and was floundering toward the air. The fact that this was my child did not sink in, and if I ever lost the child and then found it again I was not confident that I would be able to recognize it. Then I asked myself, *Would I be able to give this child unconditional love no matter what it looked like? Even if the child grew to be someone completely different from my expectations?* Those questions led to the creation of two characters who prompted me to ask this question: *If they were my children, could I love them?* That's how Yunjae and Gon were born.

Children are born every day. They all deserve blessings and to have every possibility open to them. But some of them will grow up to be social outcasts, some will rule and command but with twisted minds. Some, although very few, will succeed against all odds and grow into people who touch hearts.

I know this may be a clichéd conclusion to draw. But I have come to think that love is what makes a person human, as well as what makes a monster. That's the story I wanted to tell.

I wrote the first draft of *Almond* for a month in August 2013, when my daughter was four months old. Then I revised the draft heavily for a month at the end of 2014 and another month in early 2016. But throughout those years, the story of the two boys never left my mind. So I could say it took me over three years to write this story from start to finish.

I would like to thank my parents and my family who, thanks to their unconditional love, gave me the gift of a full heart. I once thought, and was even ashamed, that growing up in an emotionally stable condition put me at a disadvantage when it came to being a writer. As time passed, my thoughts changed. I came to realize that the unconditional love and support I'd received throughout my ordinary teenage years was a rare and precious gift, that they served as an invaluable weapon for a person, one that gave me the strength to look at the world from different angles without fear. I realized that only when I became a parent myself.

I want to thank the judges of the Changbi Prize for Young Adult Fiction who chose my work. I feel especially acknowledged to hear that there were eleven teenage judges among them. I also thank my first ever reader, H, who has read all my unpublished writings and added them to H's reading list as if they are official works. Without H's laid-back encouragement during my disappointments, I would not have been able to continue challenging myself.

And lastly, thank you to my editors at the Changbi Young Adult department, Jeong Soyoung and Kim Youngseon. You are my first friends in this new, unknown world. I am sorry if I made your work difficult at any point. It was an honor to have worked with you both.

I am not the kind of person to be actively involved in social issues. I just try to dig up stories in my heart through writing. I sincerely hope that this novel has moved people to reach out to those wounded, especially the young minds who still have great potential in them. I know this is a big thing to wish for, but I wish for it nonetheless. Children long to be loved but at the same time they give the most love. We were once all like that. I have written on the first page of this book the name of the person I love the most, the person who has given me even more love.

Spring 2017
Won-pyung Sohn

A NOTE FROM THE TRANSLATOR

"Luck plays a huge part in all the unfairness of the world. Even more than you'd expect."

When I translated these sentences from *Almond* back in 2018, I had no idea I would have experienced the power of luck myself, but in a completely opposite way. It's a rarity for Korean literature to be published in English, let alone a debut novel. Translating it was purely out of my enjoyment and half out of pressure to turn it in for a workshop. Never would I have imagined that my translation would lead to a meeting with my now-agent, Barbara Zitwer, and Won-pyung herself! And the rest is history. As much as luck plays in Yunjae's unfair world, translating his journey has given me a series of perfectly timed coincidences of luck by many helping hands who "discovered beauty" in this story. To that, as selfish as it sounds, I am grateful for Yunjae and Gon and all their misfortunes.

Portraying the series of horrific events in Yunjae's uniquely detached voice was a challenge though, especially when lining up his next to those of the other characters who are full of emotion and life, including Gon. I needed to make conscious word choices that Yunjae and Gon would use so they could equally come alive in their own unique ways, based on the context and emotional distance set from the original.

My focus for Yunjae, specifically, was ensuring he consistently sounds emotionally removed but not dull, and as a bibliophile, not less articulate in expressing his limited emotions and observations. On top of that, as Yunjae's emotional ability develops throughout the book, I wanted to show his growth through language and bridge his emotional distance. The same goes for Gon, but in the opposite way—his complex emotions needed to be in a much simpler tone due to his lack of vocabulary, not to mention his harsh language. I remember listing different swearwords for him. Surprisingly, this clash and mix of different voices are what make *Almond* fascinating to read, and for me, fascinating to translate.

In a similar vein, my other struggle was staying true to the original intent. As I made decisions between literal and liberal translation as I saw fit, I sometimes got carried away by certain word choices or phrases that might not necessarily point to the right intent. I remember having to tone down Yunjae's description of his almond routine because of the word from the original, "climax." I tried to stay vigilant not to read into the context more than what the original offers and sometimes this necessitated outside opinions. I am a reader of the book before a translator, and being a close reader, my take on the relationship between Yunjae and Gon was more than a simple friendship. There was a fine line between their love as friends and as something that transcends the conventions of friendship. As much as I valued my read of the original context, I needed to make sure as a translator my take was not overstepping the intentions of the original context. For that, I was very fortunate to have a support system of peer bilingual translators at Smoking Tigers, not to mention the thoughtful guidance from the very author, Won-pyung.

Because, to Yunjae, love is not confined in a box—he did not have any box, to begin with. I hope the English readers will feel the same rush of emotions from Yunjae's almond as I did.

Here ends Won-pyung Sohn's
Almond.

The first edition of this book was printed and
bound at LSC Communications in
Harrisonburg, Virginia, May 2020.

A NOTE ON THE TYPE

The text of this novel was set in ITC Century Light. The ITC
Century® typeface was originally commissioned for an American
magazine called *The Century* near the end of the nineteenth
century in order to make their typeface more readable. Century's
heavier hairlines and increased x-height made it a popular choice
for readers, so much so that additional designs were created as
offshoots of Century, pioneering the concept of typeface families
and making Century Expanded the first "superfamily."

HARPERVIA

An imprint dedicated to publishing international voices,
offering readers a chance to encounter other lives and other
points of view via the language of the imagination.